Maggie Graham was born in Ayrshire. She failed her eleven-plus and left school at fifteen, then worked in various factories, producing everything from bras to detonators, before marrying and having three children. She later returned to education, eventually gaining a degree in English Literature at the University of Glasgow. Since then she has worked on community writing programmes and had her work published in various journals and anthologies, including *New Writing Scotland*. Maggie Graham is the winner of the 2000 Robert Louis Stevenson Award. *Sitting Among the Eskimos* is her first novel.

Maggie Graham

SITTING AMONG THE ESKIMOS

MAGGIE GRAHAM

review

First published in 2000
by REVIEW

An imprint of Headline Book Publishing

10 9 8 7 6 5 4 3 2 1

ISBN 0 7472 7181 X

Typeset in Perpetua by
Palimpsest Book Production Limited
Polmont, Stirlingshire

Printed and bound in Great Britain by
Clays Ltd, St Ives, plc.

Headline Book Publishing
A division of the Hodder Headline Group
338 Euston Road
London NW1 3BH

www.reviewbooks.co.uk
www.hodderheadline.com

For Lauren, Cara and Steven Montgomery
and for Anne Marie and George Dickie.
still crazy

Thanks to:
Douglas Ewing
Duncan McLean, Deborah January, Peter Manson,
Janice Galloway, Andrew O'Hagan, Victoria Hobbs,
Mary-Anne Harrington and Geraldine Cooke.

Without whom this book might have remained
out in the cold.

If anyone calls you a witch,
burn for him; if anyone calls you
less or more than you are
let him burn for you.

Tess Gallagher
'Instructions to the Double'

ONE

This is the time of year when the district resounds with the sound of popping hymens. There's no danger of me adding to the cacophony; mine popped a long time ago. Anyway, mature students don't have time for bedsit passion.

I'm in the downstairs coffee bar. Wee Betty's back behind the counter, shouting, Cupuramug son? Cupuramug hen? confusing the foreign students. The place is packed with new students. Freshers, they're called, like wee sweeties. Wandering around in their stiff denim jackets and shiny Docs, lugging huge great bags for all those big important books. Give them a month and they'll all be Goths, with Peckham's carrier bags. This will be the last time I witness a mass influx of freshers. My final year. Two terms and then the finals. God, the finals. A week of hysteria, and four years over, finished. Then what?

I watch Elaine come in. She's laden with books and bags and God knows what else. She'll have aerobics or something later on. She looks lost. Then she sees me, and pushes through, balancing a mug and duntin big boys on the head with her Next duffel bag.

Hi. How ye doin? God, Lizzie, I dinnae believe we're back here.

Elaine's east coast. I'm west. And in this bloody place the two met.

She looks round at all the lost children.

Wee souls, she says.

She used to be a midwife.

I say, God, I envy them, all clean and new, with everything in front of them. I can't lose my virginity in a flat in Bank Street, to some wee wanker who spouts Sartre and Proust, and then comes in ten seconds. And not know that he's a wee wanker. And not know that the sex is lousy. And not know that he talks a load of pretentious shite. I would love to be that ignorant.

She smiles. Then asks the inevitable.

How are things?

And I press my lips together, and drag the answer up from somewhere in the region of my breastbone, where it lives.

Terrible. Now that he's at home all the time, he can object. When he was only there at weekends he didn't see. Now with this new job, he rolls in drunk and criticises. He sees me studying. He sees that the house is a tip. And now he'll see that it's Jill who's there when the kids get back from school. This year is going to be murder.

She reaches across and pats my hand.

How are the kids?

They're fine. Lisa's settled in well at secondary school.

The other two are just the same. Carrie's fighting fit, and David's driving us all daft. But they're fine. They don't suffer.

The hand squeezes mine.

I know. Of course they dinnae. Now you sit there, and I'll get you another coffee.

Her moon and star earrings tinkle when she puts the mugs down, and I admire them.

She says, They were a present. Good luck for my final year.

I ask, Who from?

She looks down into her cup and says, Martin.

Martin is the man who broke her heart when he left her after three years. He now lives with a twenty-two-year-old legal secretary.

I say, What the hell is he buying you presents for?

Oh, she says, he says that he's still part of my life. If I just hang in there, things'll be fine.

Hang in for what, Elaine? Till he stops shagging somebody else? Her eyes fill, tears brimming over, and I feel bad. I envy her too. Mine are all dammed up somewhere. I need to get out of here.

I say, C'mon. We need to move. Grant queue, bank, book shop, library. Where are you going?

She says, I've got a tutorial at three; I need to go to the library. What train will you be getting back to Saltcoats?

Quarter past four.

We arrange to meet up later. And we pick up our bags and ourselves, and we leave. We stop at the library steps and she says, Oh fuck, Lizzie, I'm scared. Are you?

Who me? Naw. Never.

And we giggle like two wee lassies. Then she goes off,

clutching Durkheim's theories on suicide. And I walk down the hill, against an oncoming tide of freshers.

The grant queue stretches for bloody miles, I'm here for the day. Two big hands grip my shoulders – Tony. I check for the volume of poetry...yes ... Rimbaud.

He says, So, auld yin, they actually let you back in.

We both like to make a big deal of the seven years between us. Exchanging insults is our way of covering up the secret we share; we shouldn't really be here. We're impostors.

Shut it, son.

He grins down at me. Then he has to say it.

Well, hen, this is it. Come April. Nine exams in eight days. Think you're up to it?

I shoot him a world-weary look.

No bother, honey. No bother.

We inch forward. A to M left – N to Z right.

He lights up a Camel, puts the packet back in the pocket of his long black coat, and asks, Who's your tutor?

I say, James Brown.

Oh, very fucking funny.

It is. Tony, stop looking at me like that, you're making me laugh. It is. It's this new guy, Dr James Brown.

Yo, Lizzie, he says, pelvic thrusting in the cloisters, Sex Machine.

I say, I wish. He looks like Ted Moult.

Who the fuck's he?

Oh forget it.

The winos are back in the lane. They probably never left; I'm the one who hibernates in summer. I've heard them.

See up at the Uni? See that wee lane? Students, overflowin wi social fuckin conscience. An the wans that drink in the fancy wine bars? A couple a bob's fuck all tae they cunts.

One of them starts jigging when he sees me.

There she is . . . Doris Day.

I say, Away to hell. She's a virgin.

And he laughs; cackling till he nearly coughs his lungs up. Then he's away again, jigging.

I'll gie ye a wee song, hen.

He stands still for a moment, getting the pose right: shoulders up, legs apart, hint of a smoulder in the blood-shot eyes, then right into 'All My Loving'. Giving it laldy. Maybe once upon a time some wee lassie believed that he'd always be true. Christ, what happened to him? One chorus, then we're back to business.

Any spare change, doll?

I say, No. I've got weans to keep.

His manner changes as he exaggerates amazement.

Oh pet, I'm so sorry. I never wid huv asked ye. Ye don't look auld enough. That's whit it wis. I thought ye wur wan a they fuckin students.

Laughing, So did I, I give him the fifty pence I had ready in my hand. And as I walk towards the Underground, I can hear him Godblessin me and my weans all the way down the lane. Then:

Hey, big man. Yer the spit a Jimmy Dean, so ye are. Any spare change?

The four-thirteen from Glasgow Central gets me home by five-thirty. In the back door. The kitchen's tidy; my domestic help is a little treasure. She makes coffee, and we compare notes — yes, they've been good — and then she goes home.

Mum, I've got the Girls' Brigade, and I hate it. And Carrie's in a huff. And Jill let David out to play and I don't know where he's gone.

She lies stretched out on her front on the carpet. Young enough still to believe that I can fix everything.

I say, Right, Lisa. Why do you hate the Girls' Brigade?

It was his mother's idea anyway. Anything to ally them with the Church of Scotland, against their papish mother.

She says, Because that woman shouts at me.

Well, don't go then. You don't need to be shouted at.

She has never needed to be shouted at.

Still not pacified, she pleads, Will you phone up? And will you tell my nana?

Yes, I'll phone up. And to hell with your nana. Now, why is Carrie in a huff?

She says, Because one of her feet's bigger than the other one.

Well, Lisa, I can't do anything about that. I'll talk to her. David's next door playing with Mark. I saw him when I came in. So, henny penny, now that we've sorted all your problems, what are you up to?

She says, I'm going down to Mandy's. She's got the new Boyzone CD.

I say, Woo. Wish I was going.

And she smiles. God, what a smile. Hang on to it, hen.

She goes away happy. And I drink cold coffee, and phone the sergeant major, and fix the huff with promises of fantastic shoes, and think, and try not to think. He's working till seven. We'll see him at ten, maybe eleven. Depends.

The kids are in bed, and I'm in this chair. I hate this bloody chair. I've got the paper. The one with the big pages, the one he hates. *Where the hell's the* Record? *Or are we too good for that now?*

My mug has COFFEE printed across it in large letters. I MUST ONLY DRINK COFFEE FROM THIS VESSEL.

Piles of books each side of me. I have everything I could possibly need beside this chair. This chair was cleverly designed to allow me to kill myself in comfort. My mother moved from a chair to a bed to a coffin without a moment's thought. I think too much, that's my trouble. I can't get comfortable.

I tried. I really tried. But when the weans stopped sharing this chair with me – the four of us, and Topsy and Tim, and Billygoat Gruff – then this chair just didn't feel right. I liked the chairs at night school. They were comfortable. Then I decided to try other chairs, see how they felt. Library chairs, lecture-theatre chairs, nice tutorial-room chairs. I'm the Goldilocks of the University, but I'm only allowed in Daddy Bear's bed. There are other chairs that I would love to try. Opera and theatre seats, train and plane seats. Yes.

I hear his key. Other men bring home fish suppers or Indian carryouts; Colin Burns brings tension, bags of it. He stands there, filling the doorway. He fills every doorway.

He says, Aye. I see you're busy. As usual.

Absence and sarcasm are his only weapons. He would never hit a woman. But if he starts tonight, I could brain him with *Twentieth Century Women Poets*; plead poetic justice.

He says, Are the weans all right?

No. They died of neglect. Of course they're all right. They're always all right.

Oh aye, he says. I forgot. You're the perfect mother.

It's just not bloody fair. But then, it never has been.

I say, How the hell would you know? You're never fucking here.

That's right, he says, get back to your roots. You were dragged up. Dae all your smart pals talk like that?

Aye.

He looms over me, reeking of diesel oil and beer. Spitting words.

What is it that you want? Eh? Go on. You tell me. What is it that you want? You don't want what other women want. You wanted weans and now you don't want them. What is it that you want? TELL ME.

God Almighty. I don't want this. I want peace. No, I don't, I want something, somebody. It used to be him.

I say, Okay. I want more than this. I want music and poetry. And I want laughter, and food, and wine. And I want to play the saxophone. And I want to go to ... fucking ... Andalusia. And I want a sober man. A sober man who loves me.

He looks down at me, and I can still see the skinny apprentice who walked me home that night. Then he says, You're no right in the heid. You are mental. You'll get they weans taen aff you. You're wired tae the moon, hen.

Someone knocks at the door. I jump up to answer it, and his mate, Wullie, stands there grinning at me.

Hello, hen. Is the big man in?

And I smile, say, Aye. Come in.

Because I'm a nice lassie. And I grab my coat, and I shout, I'm just nipping round to Bernie's. And I walk.

I walk. And I keep walking. Because I don't want to go back. I walk right down the hill, and over the railway bridge, and round past the harbour, and along the polluted shore front. It's cold, and I can smell the sea, and see the lights. And I don't care. I don't care what I see or hear or smell or feel. I just don't bloody care. The big man. The fucking big man. They even call my son wee man.

How's it goin, wee man? Pass the ba, wee man.

Nobody calls his sisters wee women.

Oh, that's a pretty dress, wee woman.

Never. When they're women, they'll get a nice wee house, a wee family, a wee part-time job, a wee night out, a wee holiday, a wee greet, a wee cup of tea. They might need a big operation, and that'll be the highlight of their wee lives. But, supposing they're ten feet fucking tall, they'll never be big women. Because, when it comes down to it, boys, size doesn't matter. Women are all wee. Next to the big man I'm really wee, and I'm shrinking by the minute. Nae bother tae the big man.

I'm still walking. Walking in a circle, because I have to go back.

Back to my big lassies and my wee man.

First tutorial with the Godfather of Soul. He opens the door before I can knock.

Come in, come in. I'm Dr Brown. Jim; call me Jim. And you are Elisabeth Burns, I take it? Do you prefer Elisabeth or Liz, or what? What should I call you?

He doesn't really look like Ted Moult, that was unkind. He's dark, heavy set, probably mid-thirties. Quite good-looking in a Heathcliffian sort of way. Heathcliffian? Christ, that's a good one. Wait till I tell Elaine.

I say, Lizzie.

He smiles, Say your name is Lizzie Borden. Show him your axe.

This could easily be my first assignment; in this place anything's possible.

I'm sorry?

A poem, he says. Tess Gallagher. 'Instructions to the Double'. You should consider it for American Lit. She was married to Raymond Carver, not that that matters. Which poets were you thinking of for that paper?

My mind immediately empties of all knowledge of American poets. It's his fault. I haven't even sat down, and he's firing bloody quotes and questions at me. I take my time, hope that I look suitably studious. Women. Think women, Lizzie.

Oh, I thought ... Emily Dickinson, Marianne Moore, and Plath.

Yes, he says, nodding.

I tense, wait for him to tell me that I can't possibly exclude Pound, Whitman, and all those other perfectly nice geniuses.

He repeats, Yes. But do take a look at Gallagher. Margaret Atwood's very interesting too. Browse around; see what you come up with.

Deprived of an argument, I say, Isn't Atwood Canadian?

Yes, he says. Doesn't mean that you can't read her.

He picks up a file from his desk, and leafs through it. I look around the room. He's certainly made himself at home: kettle, cafetiere and cups on the window ledge, radio cassette and a stack of tapes in the corner, framed photographs on the walls; Becket, Joyce and a beautiful dark-haired woman, wearing a tailored jacket and open-necked shirt.

I say, Who's she?

He looks round.

Oh, you mean Djuna. That's Djuna Barnes, another one you should read for twentieth century: *Ryder, Nightwood*, but we'll get to her later. Looking back to the file he says, So, Lizzie, Your other tutors all speak very highly of you, especially Rachel. According to her you have courage with a capital C.

I say, As opposed to Madness with a capital M?

He closes the file, and leans forward on the desk.

He says, Yes, I've no doubt there are those who think that you're certifiable. But you have kept up an amazingly high standard of work. I'm sure that you'll do well in your finals. Now, do you have an essay for me?

Yes, I have the summer vacation essay on James Joyce.

I hand it to him. Three thousand words, most of them written in the dead of night.

He says, I'm sure it's very good.

And I feel like a wee girl in primary school, giving teacher her composition. He opens the file again.

He says, I would like you to write something for the Shakespeare paper. And to save you time, I've prepared the topic for you.

He hands me a sheet of paper.

To what extent is the female shown as an instrument of tragic fate in Shakespearean tragedy?

I saw that your previous essays were pretty strong on feminist criticism, so I've given you something you can get your teeth into. Professor Sloan is lecturing on the tragedies this week, you should go along.

I would rather have malaria than spend time in the same room as that pompous bastard.

I say, No. I don't think so.

He smiles, Now, you must listen to the received wisdom before you refute it. If nothing else it will be good for a laugh. Go on, I dare you.

So. Another one of the academic groovy gang. Thank you, God.

I say, I'll try to get there but I'm promising nothing.

He comes out from behind the desk.

Fine, he says. As long as you turn up here next week with your essay, Lizzie Burns.

Right you are, Doctor Brown. Goodbye.

I walk down the stairs, and out into the quadrangle. Well well. I must ask Rachel about him.

Professor Sloan pontificates.

Of course, Volumnia was an old witch.

Of course she was. And Cleopatra was an old whore. And asphyxiation was too good for Desdemona. What the hell am I doing here?

Brave new world and what godly creatures inhabit it: Mr, Doctor, and Professor. Their footfalls echo on the same paths their forefathers trod. The names of eminent scholars are writ large in gold upon the gates, reminding us hourly.

We permit you to enter here.

Enter a world where the good doctor can proposition female freshers with tedious yet alarming regularity, and remain, tenured and unchecked. A world where the portly professor will swiftly and brutally penetrate the deepest of insecurities.

Young woman, you have no languages, scant knowledge of the classics, and an undisciplined and untutored intellect. You have no business to be in this university at all, much less the Faculty of Arts. And I will be extremely surprised if you graduate.

I fled, scattering teardrops on his hallowed halls. Running, running to nowhere, only certain that I could never go back. Running, running blindly into someone, Dr Wilton, Rachel. One of that frightening breed, the academic woman. Carelessly dressed, unadorned, armed with bulging satchel and classical education, striding sure-footed through the cloisters.

We had never met, but she took me to her room, calmed and comforted me, became my tutor and my friend. That day I left with *A Room of One's Own* and her reassurance that I would, one day, prove this corpulent wanker wrong.

The worst of it is, most of them just sit there, copying it all down. They won't reread the play, make up their own minds. No. They'll swallow everything he tells them, and regurgitate it in the finals. And they will get decent degrees.

Outside, Tony waits for me.

Was that no the biggest load of balls you've ever heard? he says.

I say, I stopped listening. Anyway, I could hardly hear for my stomach rumbling. I'm going down to the wee café in the arcade, I can't stand the queues up here.

He says, I'll come with you.

The café is quiet. Too twee for most students. Checked tablecloths and napkins can't compare with plastic knives, forks and food in the Union. The only other customer is a young girl with her baby.

We order toasted sandwiches and real coffee. And while we wait, I say, How is your work going?

What work? Tony says. I don't know if I'm going for a shite or a haircut these days. I don't know if I'm going to be able to make it, Lizzie. I'm working five nights a week in the Union, serving beer and wiping up vomit. Looking after wee prats who should be in their fucking beds. On Sundays I have to go and see my old man. He's really in a bad way, and my mother's exhausted; she can't take care of him on her own for much longer.

The baby is crying. His mother paces the floor with him. Shush, shush.

I say, Couldn't you cut back on the bar work?

Aye, I could, he says, and I could starve.

Have you talked to your advisor of studies, or the welfare officer?

He gives me a for-Christ's-sake-talk-sense look.

Those bastards couldn't care less. They're only interested in the wee Fionas and Alasdairs that overdose on Pro Plus a week before their exams, because Mummy and Daddy are expecting excellence. Nobody gives a damn about mature students in that place.

I say, You can't give up at this stage; you've put three years' work into this. There must be something else you can do.

He says, I could take a year out, sit my exams in two years. I'll see what happens with my da.

An older woman comes in with her son. He is a lumbering, retarded youth; permanently arrested in toddlerhood. She looks lined, exhausted. The boy stumbles, sends cups crashing.

He shouts, Mum Mum want juice. Mum Mum want cakes Mum Mum Mum.

She rescues falling crockery, and attempts to pacify him.

Shush, Robert. You won't get anything until you sit down and be quiet. Be a good boy now. I'll ask the lady to bring juice.

He stops and looks around. He sees the baby, and the two exchange smiles of recognition. He laughs, pointing, quieter now.

Look Mum wee baby laugh Mum Mum look.

The mothers smile too. The younger one probably thanks God for her own perfect little prince. Who knows what Robert's mother thinks? Maybe she's too tired to think at all.

I remember my babies. Remember how they ran rings round my days, and shattered my dreams at night. Remember how I loved and resented them.

Tony says, Are we off then?

We pay the bill and leave. Tony goes home. And I walk to the library, cradling books.

T W O

We sit in the wine bar, Elaine and me. We hide in here
when we want to talk. We're supposed to be going to
Lynne's birthday party. I've avoided the all-night parties
until now, scurrying home on the four-thirteen every day.

I say, Are you sure that it's okay for me to stay with you
tonight? I could easily catch the last train.

She looks indignant.

No you will not. You never get a break, Lizzie. Of
course you can crash at my place.

I can't tell her that I don't really like breaks, I'm not
used to them. And I don't crash; I go upstairs to bed,
wearing a big t-shirt, and clutching a book. And occasionally I dunt the big snoring body lying next to me.

I say, Thanks. It was lucky that he had to go up north,
and Bernie offered to take the kids. There's no way I could

have made it if he was there. Although I'm not sure that he would miss me. I could sit anybody in that chair, and he would come in pissed and criticise them. That's about all he does these days. And I always end up being nice, just to keep the peace.

Elaine says, I know. Why do we do that?

I say, It's a medical condition.

She raises her eyebrows.

Oh aye?

Aye. It's called Premature Capitulation.

She laughs. And I join in, laughing at my own joke for a change.

She says, Oh fuck. D'ye think there's a cure for it?

No. But we could try memorising Scottish Cup winners since nineteen sixty-eight.

We'd never remember, no fitba.

Quadratic equations?

Dinnae be daft, she says. We're women, we canny dae sums.

When we've calmed down, I say, Have you seen Martin?

She says, I saw him last night.

I should have known. She has that look that she always gets when he's around. Shoulders creeping up towards her ears, forehead creased in self-doubt.

She says, He's still with that bitch. And he thinks that he can pop up and see me whenever he feels like it. You were right, Lizzie. I've been a complete mug. D'ye know, I've had three years of that bastard. He was the first guy I met when I came to Glasgow. Three years of his bloody arrogance and his fucking insecurities.

I say, What did you say to him?

She grips her glass too tight.

She says, I told him to fuck off. I said that I've had

enough, that I have to get on with studying for my finals. He can go to hell.

I wonder if it is as easy as that. Just fuck off? No.

C'mon, she says. Drink up. Lynne'll think we're not coming.

We walk arm in arm the length of Byres Road. Not drunk, just affectionate. Sure you're my best pal, hen?

I dinnae ken what I'd do without you, pal. I dinnae.

Lynne's flat is crowded. There are people sitting in the hall, packed into the kitchen. We climb over bodies, and go in search of the birthday girl. She spots us and staggers over.

So you made it then? I was beginning to think you'd clicked with a couple of grey suits in the wine bar.

Elaine says, How could we? You weren't there.

Lynne giggles. True, dear, very true. You don't have my expert touch. Here. Have a drink.

She's filled glasses from a wine box on the table. I take a sip. It tastes bloody awful.

We give her presents: a biography of Garbo, and a painted wooden parrot. She collects parrots. I'm scared to ask why, in case it's something deeply Freudian. There are wooden and plastic parrots all over the flat. Stuck on to the plant pots, clipped on to the curtain poles. Even the towels in the bathroom have bloody parrots on them. Why doesn't she just get a real one?

She says, Oh, how lovely. Now I really must get back to my nice senior lecturer. He finds me absolutely fascinating.

I look over and see a woolly-looking individual gazing adoringly at Lynne. She perches on the arm of his chair, fluttering her eyelashes and flaunting her intellect. He doesn't stand a chance.

I forgot to ask if I could use her phone. Shit. I use it anyway.

Bernie answers. The kids are fine. And I've to go away and enjoy myself.

Not even a minor emergency to save me. Why couldn't Carrie have locked herself in the bathroom and refused to come out? Why does David only hang out of upstairs windows when I'm there? Oh God. What if Lisa starts her periods? Bernie doesn't know where the bag with the slimline towels and the special present – the locket with the garnet inset – is. Will she hold her, and tell her that she's a lovely girl, and that she's going to be a beautiful, strong woman?

I want to go home. *Behave yourself, Lizzie. She could take it at school and you wouldn't be there. Some teacher would give her a giant Dr White's and tell her to keep herself nice and clean.* But she would be coming home to me. I would be there at teatime.

I'm always having these arguments with myself. Maybe Colin's right. Maybe I am off my head. *Don't start that. Once you start believing them, you've had it.*

I WANT TO GO HOME.

I could still make the last train, if I got a taxi. I hate this, I feel stupid. *That's because you are stupid. Relax. These people are your friends. Elaine's only a couple of years younger than you.* But she doesn't have three weans. And I can't find her. There she is, over there, talking to that guy from Anthropology. I think his name's Nick. He's fancied her for ages. Maybe she'll go for it now, if Martin really has fucked off.

That's what I'll do. I'll just fuck off. Nobody would notice. I could go outside and stop a taxi. *That would cost a bloody fortune. And what do you mean, nobody would notice? Of course they would notice.*

I could phone up when I got home, say I felt sick. *You*

felt sick, so you travelled twenty-five miles to throw up in your own lavvy pan. Grow up, Lizzie. I am grown up; too grown up for this. And I hate bloody Teenage Fanclub.

I WANT TO GO HOME.

I look round, and he's at my elbow. Oh no. Eddie McManus, man of the people. Ex-riveter, shop steward, etc. etc. His wife divorced him for drunken slavering. And now he cultivates convenient feminist sympathies, to such an extent that you half expect to find a packet of Feminax and a box of tampons in his rucksack. He studies Sociology and Economic History, and is apt to bore the arse off anyone unfortunate enough to get landed with him.

Marx says ... Engels says ... They say fuck all, Eddie, they're deid. They may have written, but they cannot say. They're a couple of deid Germans.

He says, Well well, Lizzie. It's not often we see you out and about. What's up, has that man of yours finally consented to take on his share of the childcare?

I say, No. He's away this weekend. A friend of mine's looking after them.

Good for you, he says. A woman like you shouldn't be stuck at home, Lizzie.

He's drinking Mexican lager, straight from the bottle. Cool as fuck.

He sways a bit, and sooks his bottle through his beard.

He says, I saw you and wee Elaine in the wine bar earlier. Looked like you were having a good time. What was the joke?

Ignoring the question, I say, I didn't think you went in there, Eddie. Not turning into a champagne socialist, are we?

No way, Lizzie. No way. I was looking for big Sean. He was meeting his bird . . . eh . . . his . . . eh . . . woman.

I say, Her name is Valerie.

That's right, he says. Valerie from the gallery. She's an artist you know.

Yes, Eddie, I know.

Tony has been laughing at me for the past five minutes. Laughing and ignoring my RESCUE ME looks.

I say, You'll have to excuse me, Eddie. I see Tony over there. And there's something I really have to say to him.

He clutches at my sleeve.

Hold on a minute. There's something I really want to ask you. Been wanting to ask you for ages. Couldn't before tonight, you see.

He takes another slug and then a deep breath.

He says, The thing is ... You look like a fantastic fuck, Lizzie. Are you?

I WANT TO GO HOME.

What?

He says, You look like you'd be absolute dynamite. Can I come home with you and fuck you all night?

I say, No you cannot. You can get yourself to fuck. I don't want to see you again tonight. You are drunk, and you are lucky, because tomorrow you won't remember this conversation. I will never forget it. Now fuck off.

Oh, he says. That's what I get for being honest. I thought that was what you liberated women wanted.

I say, Go away, Eddie.

He staggers off to renew his membership of the She Done Me Wrong Party. I pour myself a very large drink. And that bastard Tony's still laughing.

I crashed, but not at Elaine's. I wake up on Lynne's sofa with some wee guy's head resting on my knee. He looks about twelve. I move him, gently. He'd probably get a bigger shock than me if he woke up. Everything's crashing; my head's crashing, and waves of nausea are crashing against my insides. I have to find the bathroom. I meet Lynne coming out, looking fresh as a daisy. She probably does this every weekend.

She says, God, Lizzie, you look terrible. I'll make some coffee.

She's right, the face I see in the bathroom mirror looks bloody awful. I have to do something; I can't go home to my kids looking like this. I use Lynne's Deep Cleansing Beauty Granules, and her Soothing Toner, and her Deep Enriching Moisture Cream. No wonder she always looks terrific; my budget runs to Pears soap and baby lotion.

In the kitchen, Lynne hands me a glass of yellow glucose stuff, and a mug with a parrot on it.

Well, she says, you were certainly having a good time last night. At one point you kept asking Tony if he thought you looked like a fantastic fuck. Are you after him?

I remember. Oh God.

I say, No, I'm not. That was Eddie.

She gives me a who's-a-naughty-girl look.

No, it wasn't, she says. It was Tony. You're not after Eddie, surely?

I say, No. It was Eddie that said it.

She hasn't a clue what I'm talking about.

Why would Eddie ask Tony if he thought he looked like a fantastic fuck? They're both straight. Aren't they? It was definitely you.

I say, Lynne, shut up. I'll tell you on Monday.

Son. See if you reach up, you could get that cobweb doon.

Colin gives me a look that says, Slut. You couldn't even clean up for our poor old widowed parents coming. And I know I should keep my mouth shut, but I can't.

I say, That's right, son. Go on, you're the big man. You could go right round the house and get them all doon.

Lisa laughs, as usual. I used to think it was nerves, but no, it's hilarity. We share a love of hilarity, Lisa and me. Like that time he took a drunken tumble down the stairs, and we ran and hid in the garden hut, laughing. Carrie isn't listening, she's watching a film. And David's building a Lego police station; bought to ensure peace today. I should have saved my money and let him run riot. My dad manages a wee affronted guffaw.

Oh my. That's awfy cheeky. She's an awfy lassie, is she no, May?

Colin's mum makes a stab at civility, twitching her lips. I can just hear her telling Auntie Annie later on.

My poor boy. Her hoose is festooned wi cobwebs, you know. Mind you, the weans are kept clean. But my Colin wouldn't have it any other way.

I squeeze in next to Carrie on the settee.

Carrie, move over, pet.

My dad tuts, sighs, then tuts again. Why dae ye cry her that? he says.

I light up before replying, Cry her what?

Her name is Caroline, he says, in the manner of one bringing news.

Carrie is listening now. She pipes up, I like being called Carrie, Grandpa.

She is ignored. Her naming is unimportant; he is concerned with his own wayward child.

He says, Her faither cries her Caroline.

That's up to him, I say. Most of the time she gets called Carrie. There isn't a problem, Dad.

He jumps to his feet, still clutching his can of McEwan's.

So you're no Elisabeth ony mair. And the name her ain faither cries her isnie guid enough fur the wean. Is that it?

I say, I chose her bloody name, for Christ's sake.

Now Colin's up on his feet as well.

Don't talk to your father like that.

Lisa isn't laughing. Carrie is glowering, fists balled at her side. David is sitting, open-mouthed, with half a police car in each hand. And May is rummaging in her bag for her heart pills.

My dad says, And your mother and me, God rest her, picked your name. And it's Elisabeth, efter yer granny, God rest her. Noo you're crying yersel Lizzie, like some hairy. You've gone aff yer heid since ye went tae that bloody college.

And there we have it. I'm aff ma heid. *Say your name is Lizzie Borden. Show him your axe.*

I say, My granny was called Betty all her bloody days. And my mother wouldn't have cared if I called myself Talullah, as long as I was happy. And it's not a bloody college, it's a bloody university. I've been telling you that for three bloody years. And I've always been aff ma heid, dad; it runs in the fucking family.

Colin's mother rises up, clutching her handbag.

Get my coat, son. I will not stay here and listen to language like that from a *woman*.

Colin gets their coats. He glares in my direction, and says, I'm taking my mother home, and then I'm taking your dad for a pint. You'd better calm down while I'm away.

The door closes and we're alone again. David comes up beside me and wipes my tears with the dish towel.

Don't cry, Mum, don't cry. It's my grandpa that's mental. Lizzie's a nice name.

Lisa hands me a glass of wine.

Here you are, Talullah.

And Carrie, muttering, Bastards, under her breath, puts *The Best of Motown* on. We manage to sit at peace through 'I Heard it Through The Grapevine' and 'My Guy', but with the first bars of 'Get Ready', Lisa's up and pulling me to my feet.

C'mon, we need to dance, Mum.

We line up, the way I taught them; David in the middle with Lisa and Carrie at either side, me at the back. Fingers clicking, three steps forward, three back, step right, clap, step left, clap, keeping in tempo. They know every lyric, every move. He's never seen us do this; we only perform when he's out. We move into a circle for The Elgins: hands outstretched, hips shaking to Mum's favourite, 'Heaven Must Have Sent You'.

So we do what we always do. We sing and we dance, and when it's over, we collapse, laughing, all of us in the one chair.

David's quite calm tonight. He has been a lot quieter since he learned to read, though. We'll soon have taken out every Roald Dahl book in the library. He brings out his homework without racing round the room. Sentences again: *Write four sentences using the word ball.* They don't have a bloody clue. No wonder the kid's disruptive; he's bored.

I sit down next to him, his hair smells of classrooms. He writes, *Today I played outside with my ball,* then scribbles down another three lines, chucks the jotter backwards over his head, and says, The teacher made me sit by myself today, just cos Melanie Duncan was cryin.

I ask, What did you do to her? dreading the answer.

Nothin, he says, a study in injured innocence. She said I was making her dizzy.

Poor wee Melanie, he's been making me dizzy for seven years.

I say, Were you walking round and round the table again?

Aye, but that should make me dizzy, not her.

He hangs upside down over the back of the chair, his arms circling wildly. He was fine until he learned to walk. Before that he fed and slept and cried and babbled, same as the other two. A normal baby, nothing out of the ordinary. Then one night I put him down in his cot – *Night-night, my darling boy* – and went back downstairs. Two minutes later he was banging on the living-room door. He had climbed out of the cot, slid down the stairs, and he made his grand entrance, attired in a double nappy and blue babygrow, smiling at us all. *Ha ha. See me?* So far, he has defied analysis. *Not clinically hyperactive, just very bright, Mrs Burns.*

I say, Oh, David, you'll need to learn to sit at peace, son.

Still suspended, he says, That's what my grandpa does all the time. He just sits and sits. You should only sit at peace when you're very old, Mum.

Maybe he's right. When my dad's not sitting in the house he's sitting in the pub, but then, that's all he ever did.

The phone rings and David runs to answer it. Mum, it's Auntie Bernie.

I thought she had an art class tonight.

Hi, Lizzie. Listen, I'm just on my way out but I wanted to ask you something. Do you think that Lisa would let me sketch her for my exam portfolio?

I say, I'm sure she would, she wouldn't be shy with you. I'll ask her when she comes in, she's down at Mandy's. You'll have to draw the other two as well though, or there will be murder.

I know, I intend to. It's just that Lisa would make such a great subject just now; still a child but on the brink of turning into a woman.

Yes, it's just a pity she couldn't turn into something simple.

She laughs, Oh c'mon, you wouldn't want her to turn into a man. I have to go now, Frank's giving me a lift. I'll see you tomorrow. Bye.

Me and Bernie have been friends for years, since Colin was Frank's apprentice. She had wee kids then. Now Linda's at college and Garry's a policeman; they've both left home. Bernie's out all the time: work, yoga, art classes, weekends away with Frank. I wonder if we'll ever get to that stage? I doubt it.

I chase David up to the shower and go looking for Carrie; she's been in her room for hours. I open the door, and Lisa's old teddy flies past my ear.

Carrie, what's up with you now?

She's lying on her bed; the floor's littered with cuddly toys.

C'mon, hen. You can have your shower when he comes out.

She sits up and folds her arms across her chest, hugging it all to herself.

Carrie, tell me what's wrong. Is it school?

Carrie doesn't find it easy, tolerating the rest of the human race.

Mum, sure you said you're supposed to love yourself? Sure you did?

Yes, darlin. You are supposed to.

I'm full of philosophical gems like that. He calls it filling their heads wi nonsense. *You'll have they weans as daft as yourself.*

Well, she says, that Kirsty Muir keeps drawing me dirty looks and saying, That Carrie Burns jist loves herself. I hate her.

I pull her close. My poor girl; the only wean in Primary 6 with a mad mother. I really want to say, Punch the silly wee bitch's face in, but I say, Don't hate her, hen; she can't help it. She's just been told the wrong stories, that's all. She'll learn one day.

Wriggling free, she says, Well, I'm not telling her the right ones, and if she does it tomorrow I'm going to kick her.

She marches out, ready to do battle for the shower, and I'm too tired to argue.

THREE

He's home early. Sitting in the chair with David beside him, flicking the remote control. Lisa's roaring, *Dad, I was watching that*. I'm sure it's a form of masturbation, all that button-pushing, he can't leave the bloody thing alone. It's been a while since I pushed any buttons for him. He's rarely sober and I'm rarely drunk. How to synchronise the urges of the dual-career couple? The piss artist and the neurotic, will they ever get it on? Not tonight they won't; I have an essay to write. When everyone else is in bed, I'll be down here, keeping company with Shakespeare.

I didn't get it finished. Five hours' sleep and then start all over again. I place books and pens on the table, my table. Not rightfully mine but one of hundreds in the library. I've claimed it as mine: my table, my chair, my degree.

Outside, the students are demonstrating. Muffled up against the cold, they stand sentry duty outside the Union and the library. Pushing leaflets: STOP TUITION FEES. STOP THE LOANS. Petitions and passenger lists for the buses to London. FIGHT FIGHT FIGHT.

I have no role in all of this; I can't fight. I take the leaflets and sign the petitions but I can't take the trip. Sometimes they pass me by, ignore my outstretched hand. She won't want a leaflet; too old, faceless, out of uniform.

Never mind, I wreak my own brand of havoc. I board the eight-thirteen to freedom every day. I abandon my husband and children and scandalise the neighbours. I am wired to the moon. My husband has no knowledge of hysteria or the tides of the menses, but he feels qualified to diagnose my condition. I am a madwoman, a malcontent, but that is a word he would never use.

The people of Saltcoats agree with him.

Her that thinks she's smart.

Whit ur ye gonny be, a brain surgeon?

Thought you'd be away on a demo, smokin dope. Heh heh.

Bastards.

Women in hooded, padded coats cross the street to avoid me. *Who does she think she is?* Hate me for snubbing the life that should be good enough for me if it's good enough for them. Even Grace has stopped popping in. *Oh, you're only reading. Stick the kettle on.* After all that time – me and Grace and five sticky, sunburned weans down at the shore. And the days when it was too wet to play, days of sheer bedlam, then a mad tidy-up when THEY were due home. In spite of all that, I had to stop sticking the kettle on.

The big man's mates fear me. They are afraid that I will lead a mass exodus of discontented housewives out of the hinterland one day; shepherd them all off to O-Level Land.

Feel sorry fur the big man, so ah dae.

So do I pal, so do I.

Get on with your work, Lizzie. I wrote until two this morning, then I crept in beside him, grateful for the warm body already there. He turned over and said, Did you get it finished? too sleepy to remember not to care. We both forgot for a while; the memory can be selective in a warm bed. We only remembered who we used to be.

Write the bloody thing. *In conclusion: Shakespeare's tragic women are victims, viragoes or whores; objects of mystification or vilification. In either case, they are deemed responsible for the fate of his 'tragic' men.*

Time for a coffee. I walk over to the Union. I spot Elaine and Sean when I go in. Elaine waves me over.

Hey, Lizzie. Either this man here's going mental, or you've got a double. He swears he saw you in Edinburgh last Friday night.

Sean stretches his long legs, then retracts them at the glower from the woman with the trolley who's clearing the tables and muttering, Dirty buggers, as she goes round.

He says, I was sure it was you, Lizzie, in Princes Street. I said to Valerie, There's Lizzie, and we waved and shouted, but you just looked right through us. We wondered what the hell was up with you.

I say, Well, it wasn't me, I was at Lynne's party. In fact, I got landed with bloody Eddie. He said he was supposed to meet you in Micha's.

Aye, he says, I changed my mind and went through to Edinburgh instead. We wanted some time, just the two of us. We had the whole weekend; went to one of her pal's showings on Saturday. It was pretty good.

He loves Valerie, never tries to hide it. Tells everybody

who'll listen, *See this woman? This is one terrific woman. I love this woman.*

The two of us. I haven't said that for so long; the five of us doesn't quite have the same ring to it.

I say, This double of mine, was she just strolling along Princes Street, all by herself?

No, she was with this big guy. Hand in hand they were; very romantic. We thought that maybe you and your man had slipped off for a wee dirty weekend.

Huh, I say, no chance. Maybe he's got a double as well. He was in Inverness while you were hallucinating in Princes Street. Are you sure you weren't tripping?

No. Straight up, he says, we'd just been for a curry.

Elaine says, Oh well, that explains it. Somebody must have spiked your vindaloo.

Or tampered with your tandoori, I say.

He grins and shakes his head at us, ha-haing all over the table.

You two are a pair of mental cases. There's one thing, Lizzie. How the fuck is the world supposed to cope with two of you?

I say, I think it would be great. My double could stay at home and do housework, and I could rent a wee flat up here; have a room of one's own. How does that sound?

Aye, he says, laughing. That would suit Eddie fine. He'd be in there like a shot, with you lookin like such a fantastic fuck, eh?

I punch Elaine on the arm, and she yelps.

Ow! What are you hitting *me* for?

I say, Because you're a big-mouth. You didn't have to tell him; it's embarrassing enough.

Sean says, You leave that wee soul alone. She didn't tell me, it was Tony. I went into the Union for a pint when I got back on Sunday, and he was working. He thought it was a great laugh. Said it was good to see you enjoying yourself for a change.

I say, Aye, that's what Eddie said, before he tried to get into my knickers.

Elaine, still rubbing her arm, says, See. I didn't tell anybody. I get the blame for every bloody thing.

Aw, hen. I'm sorry.

Honestly, it's like being at home.

She says, Well, you can stop avoiding Tony now. I don't see how you thought you were going to manage it, anyway.

Right. Enough of this hilarity. I've got more important things on my mind, Sean says. Like, has either of you two got something I can tie my hair back with? My elastic band snapped this morning, and I can't take lecture notes with my hair hanging all over my face.

Elaine rummages in her bag and comes out with a purple satin scrunchie, sending us into hysterics again.

Oh, helluva funny.

I find an elastic band. And Sean, suitably ponytailed, slopes off to his lecture.

Aw, Elaine says. He's such a nice soul, isn't he? I wonder where you get ones like that?

I don't know. What Every Woman Wants, maybe.

Oh no, that's so corny, she says. I'm going to the library before you get any worse.

Well, I'm going over to see Rachel anyway. I'll walk with you.

We walk across, through the gates inscribed with the names of renowned graduates: men of letters. Elaine goes into the library and I walk across the quadrangle and climb the stairs to Rachel's room.

I knock. She calls out, Come in.

She sits facing me, partly obscured by stacks of papers and piles of books. She says, Hi, Lizzie, I'm a Mama.

And I think, She has totally lost it.

I read it in the *Guardian*, she says. It's the same sort of idea as Yuppie, only it stands for Mothering Academic with Multi Abilities. I thought to myself, Oh, that's all right then. I will hold that thought close to my heart the next time I have a pile of marking, a week of lectures and seminars to prepare, a daughter with measles and a husband who's buggering off on tour again.

She pours coffee from the machine in the corner.

I laugh, Elinor doesn't really have measles, does she?

No, but she did when Peter was in Boston. And he's going to Budapest next week, so she's probably incubating chickenpox at this very minute.

I wish my beloved would bugger off to Budapest. But somehow I can't quite picture Colin with a cello clasped between his knees. Rachel's husband plays with the Scottish National Orchestra.

So, how about you? Rachel says. How have you been?

Me? Oh, I'm wonderful. I just recently had a battle with my father because I dared to shorten my name and, even worse, allowed my daughter to shorten hers. You know, how dare I mess around with the names we were given? Disregarding the fact that we always have a man's name, whether our father's or our husband's, it is now a hanging offence to call yourself whatever the bloody hell you please. I'm toying with the idea of emulating HD, Hilda Doolittle. I'll use only my initials and eliminate my female identity entirely, see how that grabs him. It's a good job Willa Cather never had the same idea.

She laughs and tops up our coffees.

Just what you need to kick off your final year, Lizzie. And what do you think of your new tutor?

I say, He comes across a bit brusque at first, but yes, he's okay, I think we'll get on. Thank you for the recommendation, by the way.

Rachel smiles. Hardly undeserved, Lizzie. You should work well with Jim; he's a far cry from some of the Neanderthal types you encounter in this place. I've known both him and his partner, Anna, for years. She teaches Women's Studies at Strathclyde. Between you and I, there is a reason for his apparent brusqueness. Years back, he had a fling with a mature student, a married woman. It ended very messily. He almost lost his job, and Anna. They parted for a time but she took him back. He learned his lesson, did our Jim, and ever since he's been wary of his female students.

Well, I hope you told him that I have neither the time nor the inclination for a torrid affair, with him or anyone else.

Rachel pushes a wisp of hair back behind her ear and leans back in her chair. I told him that you are a sound and sensible woman, she says.

Oh, gee, ta, Rachel.

I rise from my chair and go over to the bookshelves that line the walls of her room.

Can I still borrow these, even if you're no longer my tutor?

You don't need to ask, she says. Take whatever you want.

Last year I borrowed books from these shelves on a weekly basis. Books to read on the train or late at night when the house was silent. My reading rarely coincided with essay topics. Random selections: lit crit, biography, revived feminist classics. I read in order to immerse myself, however briefly, in this world, Rachel's world. Tasting from her books, as I would like to taste from her life. I hold up two titles: *The Second Sex* and *The Madwoman's Underclothes*.

I'll take these, I say. They'll go down a bomb with the boys back home.

There's a timid little knock on the door. She jumps up.

Shit. That's my two o'clock tutorial. Where the hell is his essay?

She rifles through her briefcase.

Here it is. More puerile nonsense on Lawrence. Some of these young men have the strangest ideas about women. I pity all those females out there, encountering self-styled priests of love in the Union every Saturday night.

I gather up my things, ready to leave. She puts her arm around my shoulders.

Pop up again soon. In fact, I'll bring lunch in next Tuesday, if you can make it.

I say, Yes, Rachel, that would be great. About one?

Yes, she says. Would you tell Paul to come in? That is if he hasn't taken fright and run off. Take care, Lizzie. Don't let them get to you.

Paul is an anaemic-looking wee person with a very long fringe. He squints and blushes when I speak to him. I make my way down the stairs and out into the quadrangle. The air is cold, and I scuff through fallen leaves. Soon these trees will be bare, and then it will be Christmas. Christ, I can't cope with Christmas.

Bonfire night. David is overexcited for days beforehand.

Can we go, Mum? Can we? Say honest. If you say honest that means we have to go, doesn't it, Mum? We can go, sure we can?

The Ardrossan Knights of the Round Table organise the event, cordoning off the area round the harbour, the safety zone where the bonfire will be lit. They are out in force with the collection cans on Saturday afternoon, the only time they're likely to catch more that a dozen folk in the main street in Saltcoats. We've been coming to the firework display for years now, except for the times when they were babies. Then I was left behind with only the wee one to care for. I liked that, and I was always pleased to see them when they came home, all rosy-cheeked and wide-eyed with wonder. No more babies.

We jump down on to the sand, leaving the more sober Saltcoats citizens lining the pier. Lisa takes my hand, and Colin holds Carrie close at his side. There's no point in attempting to hold on to David. He's jumping around us, a small pagan in a duffel coat, scarf and gloves, summoning fire and light. He stops for a second, then tugs at my arm.

Ha ha ha. Look. The bonfire, the bonfire. Ooh look.

Everyone looks, as rockets and whizzers fly upwards into the sky, shower into light reflected in the dark sea, and then fall, cascading on to the waves. Colin picks David up and heaves him on to his shoulders. The man next to us takes an exaggerated step back.

Oh my, son. That's a helluva height yer up.

We all laugh. I look at the girls. Carrie, eyes shining, snuggled up to her dad, and Lisa looking round to see who she can see. Next year she'll want to come with her pals.

From his vantagepoint, David is waving his arms and shouting.

I can see Uncle Frank and Auntie Bernie. YO, AUNTIE BERNEEE.

They come towards us, stumbling arm in arm across the sand.

Hi kiddo, Frank says. You can always hear this boy before you see him.

Bernie's kissing and hugging us all, laughing up at David. Craning her neck, a full five feet two on her tiptoes.

My God, Colin, was that the only way you could get my laddo here to stay at peace?

We all ooh and ah as the sky lights up and sparks shower into the sea. David calls out to his wee pals from school, and Bernie takes my arm, and Frank hugs the lassies close and I look up at Colin, holding our son secure. I never want to lose this. I don't need student parties; I need this.

I turn to Frank and Bernie.

I didn't expect to see you two here tonight.

Frank says, Are you kidding? I thought all this would stop when the weans grew up. But no. Yer pal here was gibbering like a budgie by five o'clock the night. Aw, Frankie baby, c'mon, honey bun, let's go and see the big bootiful bonfire.

He imitates Bernie's luvvy-duvvy voice, making the kids giggle. Bernie sticks out her tongue at him and makes them worse. He turns to Colin.

I'm no kidding you, big yin. I've been mairried for twenty-five years tae a bloody muppet, and she's got me as daft as herself.

Colin grins and shakes his head, jiggling the wean.

And there was me thinking that thirteen was enough fur ony man.

The show's ending. People begin to drift away.

Bernie says, Well, it looks like that's it then. Listen, we're going to the Chinky's. Why don't we all go? Have the weans had their tea?

Carrie looks at me as if to say, Mum, you said we weren't to say that. And I pray that she won't deliver a lecture on political correctness.

I say, No. We were going to take them for chips. Colin, what do you think?

I know that if he says no, it will be because he intends to slip off for a pint, and that I'll want to kill him if he does. The kids are shouting.

Aw can we, Dad? Please please please.

And he has no option but to give in gracefully.

Aye, okay. But you lot better behave. I mean it.

We will. We will.

Lisa flounces on in front, confident that injured airs will get her everywhere.

Honestly, Dad, I'm nearly thirteen.

We opt for the restaurant with the terrible decor and the decent food, as opposed to the one with the fancy decor and the lousy food. The other one has piped oriental music. This one plays Hits of the Seventies selections.

A variety of dishes arrive, owing to Frank having made an executive decision.

We'll just have a wee bit of everything, he says.

Aye, Frank, whatever you say.

David sits between Frank and Colin, and the combination of food and having two adult males to answer his constant questions is enough to keep him seated. Bernie and I carry on with the girls, swapping bits of food and giggling.

I wonder how Elaine's getting on. That guy Nick was going round for dinner tonight. They've already been out a couple of times. Maybe tonight's the night. She phoned earlier, in a panic because she'd made a pavlova for dessert and it had spread all over the oven.

Christ, Lizzie, by the time he gets here I'll be marooned in a sea of meringue.

I wasn't much help to her; I couldn't speak for laughing. I don't know if I could cope with being single. One minute broken-hearted over one man, and a bag of nerves over another one the next. But I suppose having kids would eliminate intimate dinners for two.

Colin looks round at the kids.

You would think these three hadn't been fed for a week.

Bernie puts her arms round the girls and winks at David.

They're growing weans, so they are. And you're not exactly a picky eater yourself, mister. I'm just glad to see their mother sitting down to a meal for a change. What this lassie eats wouldn't keep a sparrow going.

Frank and Colin launch into their usual double act.

Don't you believe it, Bernie. There's many a time I've caught her having a three-course meal at four in the morning. She just likes folk to feel sorry for her.

The kids collapse in hysterics. And Frank's right on cue.

Aye, you only have to look at her, she must be at least eighteen stone.

I say, Oh, very funny. You two are just jealous because I've kept my figure, and you've got a great pair of beer bellies there. The money that's been poured into those guts could buy a row of houses.

Colin says, Speaking of beer, why don't we grab some cans and a bottle of wine for you two and head back to our place?

Bernie leans across the table and pokes him in the chest.

Excuse me. A bottle?

Okay okay, he says, one and a half bottles.

The men go up to pay the bill and buy the booze, as men do in these parts, while Bernie and I get the kids organised. David makes pths-pths noises when Bernie dampens her napkin and scrubs his face. There's a minor panic over lost gloves. But soon we're all ready, and heading home.

It is after two when Bernie and Frank leave. Colin bought whisky as well as beer, and he and Frank are well gone. Frank stops on the doorstep, his hands on Bernie's shoulders, winking at Colin.

I could be wrong, big man. But I think I'm on to a promise here.

Well, son, Bernie says, it's no often you're right but you're wrong again. I'm in no fit state to cope with brewer's droop the night.

Frank turns back to me and cups my face in his hands.

Sure you love me, darlin? My flower of the burnin desert. And I love you. Don't you ever forget it. And you, big yin. Kent you since you were jist a couple of weans. Remember? Well, just don't ever forget it. Me and the wee barra here, we love you.

Bernie's standing on the top step with her hands on her hips.

C'mon, you daft bastard. Oh my God, would you look at him? He's like a wee rubber man. It's a good job we're just round the corner. Come on, you, move it. Night, hen. Night, Colin. Thanks, I've really enjoyed myself. It was a lovely night.

I go straight up to bed when they've gone. I am so tired; sea air and Liebfraumilch is a lethal combination. I check on the weans. Carrie has kicked her quilt off and I cover her up. Earlier, she said, Auntie Bernie, sure it would be great if Madonna was your auntie?

What? Bernie said. My auntie, hen?

No, she said, a wee girl's auntie. I mean, if she was your

mum or your big sister you'd be dead affronted. But if she was your auntie, sure it would be brilliant?

Bernie has promised to dress up as Madonna next Halloween. She's wonderful. They both are. Frank is so good with David, he's so patient with him.

I'm in bed by the time my husband manoeuvres the stairs. He falls across the bed, trapping my legs, and lies there, mumbling into the quilt.

Aye, up here to get away from me. Hoped I'd fall asleep, eh? Don't want me. Don't need me. Got yer smart pals. I'm no good enough. Is that it? Just the big, soft bastard who pays the bills. Well, I'm off. Monday. Inverness. Taking the job. That suit ye? Rid of me. Telling you. Somebody wants me.

Colin, I say, I've always wanted you but you were never here. Colin, do you hear me?

He's asleep. My only reply is a loud snore.

FOUR

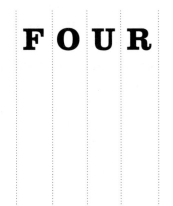

I walk out into the cold after Rachel's lecture on the Brontës. Great stuff, especially on *Villette*. I'm sure that someone else was supposed to be doing those lectures this term, I must remember to ask Rachel when we have lunch tomorrow.

I hear someone calling my name.

Lizzie? Lizzie, hang on a minute.

It's Tony. He comes running towards me, breathless and dishevelled. He was late for the lecture. But then, he's always late for lectures. He stands in front of me, looking puzzled.

He says, What are you doing here?

What the hell are you talking about?

Well, he says, I saw you getting on a train at Queen Street this morning.

I say, Tony, as you well know, I don't get on trains at Queen Street in the mornings. I get off them at Central. What's up with you?

He says, I know it sounds daft, but I was so sure that it was you. I got a helluva fright when I saw you just now.

First Sean and now Tony. I must really have a double. Unless they're fixated with me, and so they keep seeing me everywhere. No, that's stupid.

Mind you, he says, I did think that you were looking kinda dolled up, not in your usual kinda get-ups.

Meaning that I normally look like something that fell off a flittin?

No, Lizzie, he says, I didn't mean that. Don't be so fucking touchy. It's just that this woman had, like, high heels and stuff that you don't usually wear. But I swear to God, she was your absolute double.

Was she with anybody?

Aye, he says, a big tall guy.

A big tall guy. That's what Sean said too. Colin was in Queen Street this morning. We travelled up together, said goodbye in Buchanan Street, then he went for his train. Who is she? She can't be me. No. Stupid.

I say, Are you winding me up? Is Sean behind all of this? Because if you two are at it, I'll kill you.

No, honestly, Lizzie. Sean did tell me about seeing you in Edinburgh that time, and then it turned out it wasn't you at all. But I've got better things to do than piss about inventing stories at this time of the morning. I really did think I'd seen you.

We walk across to the coffee bar. I'm still pondering. Could it have been Colin? But it wasn't me, so what the hell am I on about?

Tony finds a seat while I get the coffees. When we're

sitting down, I say, What were you doing in Queen Street station this morning anyway?

He says, I was up at my sister's in Stirling last night; it was my wee nephew's birthday. My old dear makes us go to these things, and I usually go up to see her and my dad on a Sunday, so we were all up at our Donna's. I stayed the night and caught a train this morning.

That's nice, I say. What age is your nephew? Which one was it?

Luke, he says. He's four, and Jonathan's six. I'm not kidding you; those kids have got everything. Linda and Alan are so bloody materialistic: the house, the car, the stuff those kids get. Everything has to cost a fucking fortune. Me and Donna used to get on really well, but now she's just another boring middle-class housewife. All she talks about is the price of things. And the kids are a pair of ruined, cheeky wee bastards. If they were mine I'd kick their arses.

Another man who thinks that he could do it better. He should ask some single parent who's living on income support if she'd swap places with his sister. Only the unencumbered find parsimony attractive. I suppose his weans will be reading bloody Kerouac when they're four, and reciting Shelley every night before bed.

Here, in Rachel's room, with her daughter's drawings on the wall, and the coffee poured, I can relax. I'm finding the constant crush in the cafeteria very hard to cope with these days.

I remember the Brontë lectures.

Rachel, I say, why are you doing the Brontë lectures this term?

Didn't you know? she says. Clare Lewis is on maternity leave.

No, I didn't. When's the baby due?

Beginning of February, I believe. Clare's gone back home to Oxford. I'm the only woman left in the department now. God help me.

I bite into a sandwich; wholegrain bread and egg mayonnaise. I hate egg mayonnaise. There's apples to follow; apples make my teeth ache.

She goes on, They haven't found anyone to replace Clare yet, so I'm saddled with some of her lectures. Lizzie, do you ever feel so bloody tired that you simply want to crawl into bed and stay there?

I look, smile, and nod.

Oh, how bloody stupid. Of course you do. Sorry, Lizzie, I'm just completely exhausted. My mother is staying with us, and she's becoming increasingly dotty. It's so bloody wearying, repeating yourself over and over again, and having to be constantly vigilant in case she harms herself. And she can't be left alone with Elinor. I feel like I have two four-year-olds. She's going to have to go into a nursing home, very soon.

I try to imagine putting my dad in a home. The very thought is enough to make me squirm. We don't do that where I come from. We take care of our own where I come from. What's the matter with me? It isn't Rachel's fault. None of it is Rachel's fault. She has a husband, a child, an elderly, ailing mother and a demanding job. The woman's tired, for God's sake.

I say, It's only a few weeks to the Christmas break, Rachel. If you can last out until then you'll be fine.

Yes, she says, I'm really looking forward to it. We're going away this year. Some friends of ours have rented a house in Tuscany. There'll be fourteen of us in all, eight adults and six children, so Elinor won't be lonely. I can't wait to simply sit and relax in the sun.

She's going to leave her mother alone in a nursing home at Christmas. Bloody hell. I don't know what to say to her, and I can't face any more food. I busy myself rummaging around in my bag for her books.

I brought these back, I say. Thanks.

I place the books on her desk. She moves them aside and begins cutting up apples with a little knife she has brought.

She says, Help yourself if you want any more.

I don't know if she means books or food. I don't want either of them. I don't know what I want. I feel sick, probably the sandwich. God. I stand, pick up my bag, and I lie to her.

Rachel, I'm so sorry. I've just remembered that David has a dental appointment today; I have to go now. Sorry about lunch. Maybe we could do it some other time. I'll bring the food.

Her desk is cluttered with coffee cups, apple cores and paper towels. The sandwich box is still half full. You are an ungrateful bitch, Lizzie. She walks me to the door.

It's a shame that you have to dash off, Lizzie. We will do it again. Although, with things being so hectic, I'm not sure when. I'll call you at home sometime.

I leave her, and I walk down the avenue, in the opposite direction from the library and the coffee bars and the Union. I walk down the lane, past the bistros and the winos. I walk towards the Underground with the wintry wind in my face.

I'm going home.

Dr James Brown, Jim, Jamsie Bhoy, Emmae Peeaitchdee, Godfather of All the Wee Souls, lover of the woman who spreads the word, heartstease of the woman who was not his, Englishman abroad, pedagogue of the broad who must learn the literature of his language his way; carelessly drips scorn on her writings on the writings of that other great James, Jim, Jamsie Bhoy, who hailed from a much closer farther land.

Your essay on James Joyce, he says. It's well written, but . . .

But?

Yes, well, I'm afraid it's rather limited.

He has music playing. Bloody God-awful music. A cacophony of discordant sounds. I've never heard anything like it.

Resisting the temptation to reply, Och, your arse, I remain within the much less colourful confines of his own mother tongue.

I say, I don't think so. In what ways do you find it limited?

He says, Lizzie, your study of *Ulysses* concentrates almost exclusively on the character of Molly Bloom. The examiners won't like it.

I say, The examiners aren't getting it. It is an essay, my essay. What the hell have the examiners got to do with it?

He searches about his person for his patience, laid down when the last student left. The musical distraction continues, like a squadron of two-year-olds let loose in an orchestra pit.

You know perfectly well that if a question comes up in the finals paper which does not allow you to draw on the work you have here, then your answer will be limited. And it will be marked accordingly. That is what I meant, Lizzie.

I say, And if I attempted to write an essay on *Ulysses* in its entirety, I would be a professor by the time I got out of this place.

For God's sake, woman, I'm trying to help you. Will you just listen?

Listen? He has got to be kidding. If he doesn't turn that tape off I'll go berserk.

I say, Just a minute, Jim. What the hell is that?

What is what?

That music. That bloody awful noise blasting from your cassette player.

Oh, he says, jumping to his feet. I'm sorry. You don't like it?

I hate it. It's like the soundtrack to a nightmare. What is it?

He hits a button, and, mercifully, it stops.

It's Stockhausen, he says. You're supposed to find it thought provoking, stimulating.

I feel my face burning, the flush creeping up from my neck.

I'm sorry. You didn't tell me I was *supposed* to. Will I be expected to write an essay on it?

He winces.

I'm very sorry, Lizzie. I didn't mean to sound like such a complete prat. I get carried away with my enthusiasms and expect others to share them. Can we start again? Would you like a coffee?

Oh, for Christ's sake. He's a nice man. It's up to you. You can stay, behave like a grown-up, and get on with the bloody work. Or, you can stomp off in a huff, all lopsided from the bloody great chip on your shoulder; hirple back to Saltcoats and a lifetime of house-wifery.

Yes. Thanks.

He makes the coffee, and changes the music: Schubert. See, I know that one. I take a scalding sip before telling him.

Listen, about the essay. I didn't have time to work on the whole of *Ulysses*. I had the kids all summer, and I couldn't trail them all the way up here to the library. I did as much as I could, and I know I can't expect to be treated any differently from your other students—

Yes you can, he says. Believe me, Lizzie, you can. I have students who are writing the summer essay as we speak; students who were travelling or working or just enjoying themselves and not giving a damn. You, however, do give a damn. *And*, you have responsibilities.

He rifles through a pile of papers on his desk and extracts some photocopied sheets.

He says, After I read your essay I copied these for you. They're critiques on *Ulysses* and Joyce in general. When you have time, read them over; I've highlighted the relevant passages. Your essay was *good*, Lizzie, these will simply allow you to expand on it in the exam.

Thank you, I say. I'm very grateful.

He shakes his head. In wonder or in sorrow?

I don't want or deserve gratitude, he says. Believe me, I was not getting at you earlier. My job is to ensure that you get your degree. Just let me help you, Lizzie, it's what I'm here for.

Mortified, I gather up my things, ready to leave.

He continues, I want you to make a start on the Victorian paper as soon as possible. How about Hardy?

God no. His heroines all end up hanged or drowned or sold with their children. Rachel's doing the Brontë lectures next week; I'd prefer to start with them.

Fine, he says. Although I haven't prepared a topic for you.

That's okay. I'll take one from my lecture notes.

I head for the door, desperate to leave. Wanting to get out, away from this room, away from this man. This kind man who plays avant-garde music in his tutorials, only to be slagged off by wee Mrs Huvnie a Clue.

Turn aaf that pish. Huv ye no goat ony Dolly Parton?

Standing, he begins scribbling on a note pad. He tears off the page and hands it to me.

There's a list of crits you might care to look at. Rachel will probably cover most of them, but if you can get some background reading in first it will be helpful.

I glance at the paper, seeing nothing, before cramming it in to my pocket.

Thank you. I'll see you next week. Goodbye.

He comes round the desk, opens the door for me.

Oh, and Lizzie, watch out for the rage.

Pardon?

He says, In the novels. Read what Virginia Woolf had to say. She thought that *Jane Eyre* in particular was marred by female rage. Interesting point; see what you think. I'll look forward to discussing it with you.

Is he laughing at me?

I head straight up the hill to the library in search of the crits. This next essay had better be bloody perfect.

I bump into Elaine in the library.

Come for a drink before you go home, she says. I have so much to tell you, I haven't seen you since last week.

I sit, waiting for her to bring me an elegant glass of wine, chosen from the blackboard on the wall, served by the barman with the Navajo hairdo and the cute bum.

I call Jill. Would she mind? Next train?

No, don't be daft. I'll give them their tea. Okay, I'll just stay for mine. You take as long as you want, we've got a video. See ye.

Elaine settles herself beside me, her coat and bags in a pile at our feet. Sometimes she reminds me of a very well-dressed wee bag-lady, carrying her worldly goods around the West End.

I say, Right, tell me all about Nick. What happened last Saturday? Does he wear pants or boxers? Is it big or wee? Straight or curved?

Well, she says, Saturday night was wonderful. Pants. Medium but chunky. Straight. And, you didn't ask, but . . . big balls. And it was really good. No nipple tweaking. Didnae attempt tae sandpaper my clitoris, or swing my legs roon his neck. The boy done good. No, honestly, it was really nice and funny and . . . Oh, you know, just *good*.

I hope she isn't falling in love, I don't think I could cope.

But, she says, wait till I tell you. Sunday afternoon, we were still in bed, doing all that daft stuff with the papers and the radio and the never-ending nookie. And guess who came to the door?

I say, Martin?

Aye, she says, I went to the door in my t-shirt and knickers. And I said that he couldn't come in, it wasn't convenient. He went away with a face like fizz. Then, on Monday night I was lying around, completely knackered, and he appeared again. Do you know, the bastard had actually come round to interrogate me? He demanded to know who the guy was, and just what did I think I was doing? The whole bloody injured-ego trip.

I feel like I'm living in a novel. I have never experienced anything like this; my love life was never this interesting. When your first wean comes along six months after the wedding, you only experience passionate scenes and never-ending nookie second-hand. *Tell me your stories, girls.*

She says, He said that he had come round on the Sunday to try to sort things out with me. That I had known that he needed some space after he left her. But he was ready to try again. And now I had ruined everything.

What did you do? I say. I hope you booted his arse right out the door.

Well, she says, it was weird. I just felt this calmness come over me. Martin was this ludicrous man that I had mistakenly let into my life. Standing there, all red in the face, still convinced that he could reduce me to a gibbering wreck. It was pathetic.

So, what did you do?

Oh, Lizzie, it was so funny. I sat there and I thought, Fuck this. I need to dance. And I jumped up, hit the button on the CD player, and Otis Redding came on. And I just bopped all over the sitting room, shut my eyes and jumped and jived and strutted my stuff. It was brilliant.

The novelist and the playwright and the bit-part actor interrupt their self-congratulatory conversation at the bar, and observe the two hysterical females in the corner.

And he just stood there. And then he said, *Call me when you have regained your sanity. I am very worried about you, Elaine.* And he left. Old sober suit fucked off, and I didn't care.

I say, Oh, Elaine. Otis Redding? Was it 'Mr Pitiful'?

We will likely pop up one day in a macho, gritty Scottish television drama, or a macho, gritty but poetic Scottish novel. She'll shag the hard man with the heart of gold. And I'll be found deid up a close.

Another couple of glasses. That barman is a beautiful boy.

I ask, Are you seeing Nick this weekend?

No, she says, I'm going home. My mother wants to go Christmas shopping.

I say, I haven't even thought about it, I'm waiting till the end of term. I know what the kids want. But everybody else will just have to take what they get.

My mother is always very organised, she says, she only

has mine to get. So we're going through to Edinburgh on Saturday. I'll pick clothes or something, and we'll go for a meal. Then I'll go back home with her; see the rest of the family.

You'll probably see me in Edinburgh, copulating at the top of Scott's monument or something.

What?

I say, Remember Sean said that he thought he saw me in Edinburgh? Well, Tony spotted me in Queen Street station, wearing stilettos, and I was with a big tall guy, again. I wasn't anywhere near Queen Street station, but Colin was there at that time on Monday. It's bloody surreal.

Dinnae be daft, she says. If it wasn't you, then it wouldn't be Colin. Are you sure Tony isn't winding you up?

I thought that too. But he was genuinely surprised to see me at the lecture, he was so sure he'd seen me teetering up the platform in my high heels.

But, Lizzie, you wouldn't be caught deid in high heels.

I say, I know, so does Tony. But he was convinced that it was me. I don't know, but after Tony said it, I felt weird. As if this whoever she is really does have something to do with me. Maybe Colin's made himself a wee Stepford Wife, and he just hasn't got round to killing me yet.

Elaine's brow wrinkles into a wee worried frown.

You've been under too much bloody pressure. Forget about it. You know what guys are like, one good-lookin blonde's like all the rest. Anyway, Colin widnae dae that till after Christmas; you've still got all that shopping to do. Another glass of wine, Lizzie?

The kettle exploded this morning. It is a conspiracy to hold me back, keep me here, housebound. Even inanimate objects are against me. Are kettles inanimate? I know they are. But what about all those currents running through them? Is an electric kettle electric?

It wasn't actually the kettle, it was the socket. A bang and blue flashes shooting from the socket. I stood there, worried that my life was about to end, yet not worried about my life or myself. My life did not flash before my eyes, I did not think, Oh no, I haven't seen the pyramids, or, I've never had a multiple orgasam, or even, The only beach I have ever seen is bloody shitty Saltcoats shore. I didn't worry about my limited life. I worried about my children. I constantly worry about them, but this worry is peculiar and, well, worrying. Potentially lethal volts flashed inches from my vulnerable body, and I thought, The children. The children will find me lying dead. It will ruin their lives. I can't die. It wouldn't be good for the children.

My life is not my own. I never take risks, for the self-same reason. I always cross at the green man. I never walk alone in the dark. I sit in the middle carriage on trains, as a crash is more likely to affect the front or the back carriages. I am vigilant in my care of my children's mother.

Will it always have to be this way? When I am old, will I fear or welcome death? Or will I fear the effect on my middle-aged children, should they find me undignified and lifeless on the living-room carpet? Or will they be living in other countries, other continents, and have to take the telephone calls that will tell them that their mother is dead? How shocking.

Today has been bad. First the kettle and then Lisa trailing downstairs like an adolescent Ophelia; white-faced and frightened of her female malady. Oh, Mum, I don't feel well.

I couldn't leave her. My mother took me to the doctor at that age. Then, we were said to be in need of a tonic. Lisa is in need of a mother. Her periods began yesterday. And all the loving affirmations in the world won't change the fact that she is ill and scared and feeling powerless to change what has happened to her. What will happen to her?

She is sleeping now, wrapped up in a blanket on the settee where I can watch her. The baby whose downy hair I used to nuzzle with my chin when I held her. Tracksuits have replaced her tiny dresses and soft knitted jackets. But she is still the same child, my child. The same child, the same heart-stopping love and heartbreaking guilt. Always the guilt. Guilt for loving her and guilt for leaving her. Guilt when I go there and guilt when I stay here. I won't study today. More guilt. I will have to see Jim and tell him that this essay will also be rather limited; limited to about ten pages. Still, I won't study, and I won't clean the house either. It's amazing how the guilt mounts up, isn't it?

I miss my mother. She should be here. The weans never knew her; they've only seen photographs. In those she is young; she will always be young. She would be sixty now. I wonder how she felt about dying and leaving me?

I tried to make it easy for her. I found a replacement, a husband, and then I became the mother. Don't worry, Mum. I'll be fine.

FIVE

The way is clear. I will have to get myself organised. Lists. I need lists. There is so much to do. David is to be a shepherd in the school nativity play. They all need new clothes for their Christmas parties. I have to buy presents and order a bloody turkey, clean the house, find the tree, send the cards. Too much to do, far too much to do.

I can't find any paper to write my lists on. A bloody student with no paper. Christ, you're neither use nor ornament, Lizzie. Right. Lists. I don't know where to start. I should be writing an essay, or a poem, or a novel. How many women have written endless lists instead of master-pieces?

I have to make David's costume, and I can't sew. I could staple it together. Would that make me a bad mother? If my son turns up on the day, wearing a brown curtain, stapled at the seams, will the jury of professional mummies find me guilty of gross neglect? Would David consent to wearing such a creation? Probably not.

The end of term piss-up is tomorrow. I don't have time to go. Elaine and Tony have been pestering me all week.

Come, Lizzie. Ditch the guilt. Christ, it's a night out, no an orgy.

Oh Lizzie, try to make it. I can't take the piss out of everybody on my own, can I? You'll be there, pal, sure you will?

A night in the pub, a wee night out. Just what I need.

My dad sits facing me. He is not a happy man. I don't know if he has been happy at all since she died, although he gives a good impression. Life and soul of the party, would sing at the drop of a bunnet, would Tam. Shouts the numbers at the bingo nights in the Labour club, MC at the Saturday socials.

Best of order now. Wan singer wan song.

But is he happy? Right now, he is far from happy with me.

He has always found me a bit of a puzzle. Me with my head stuck in a book, sitting on the back steps while the other weans played rounders or hide and seek. Me swathed in old curtains, dreaming up palaces and royal courts, and playing all the roles myself. And when I was older. Mini skirts, black eyeliner, and too bloody cheeky by half. He still can't make head nor tail of me. *Whit the hell is she playing at?*

He says, So you managed to fit me in, eh? I canny mind the last time you came round tae see me. Too busy, I suppose. I never see you these days.

I say, Dad, that isn't true. I can't run down here all the

time, with Colin being away. I had to get a babysitter tonight. It isn't easy for me, on my own with the weans all the time. Lisa hasn't been very well, and I've got everything to do for Christmas. I really don't have a lot of spare time, you know.

Oh aye, but you've time tae run up and doon tae Glesga every day of the week. I don't understand you. When are ye gonny stop this nonsense? I worry about you. Can you no see?

Somehow, this worrying about me feels insulting. Why worry about a grown woman who is making her own choices and not harming a bloody soul?

He says, You know, hen, you'll need tae watch. Colin won't put up with all this carry-on of yours for ever. You'll lose him. Many a man would have put his foot doon before this. That man works all the hours God sends for you and they weans, if you're no careful he could mibbe find somebody that would appreciate him. Naebody could blame him if he did.

Is that right, Dad? Naebody could blame him? Well, I could blame him. I could blame the bastard for not appreciating what he has. Me and three beautiful weans, that's what he has. Oh, I could blame him. I could blame you too; you and the rest of the small-minded folk who constantly put me down. I've done nothing wrong. I haven't hit the drink or the pills, I'm not running around with other men. I'm studying for a degree, that's all. And that's a good thing, Dad, a bloody good thing. Why can't you just be proud of me? My mother would have been.

He straightens the embroidered cloth on the wee table at his side, folds the paper, opens and closes his spec case. Restoring order. He's thinking. I've watched him before, standing motionless with a plate in one hand and a dishtowel in the other, working out whatever's wrong with his world.

Aw, hen, he says, don't upset yourself. I'm sorry. You're right, she would have been proud of ye. You're like her, and I don't suppose she got tae dae all the things she wanted. I jist want ye tae be happy. I ken wan thing, it's nae fun being on your own. All these years, and I'd dae anything tae huv her back. I'm sorry I said whit I did. I'm jist that feart that ye end up on yer own.

He's up on his feet, closing the curtains, putting the cups in the sink.

I'm gonny take a wee stroll round tae the club. Huv ye got time for a drink before ye huv tae get hame?

A peace-offering. The only kind he has to give. Can he buy me a wee half?

Aye, I say, but it will need to be just the one.

Right, get your coat on. Christ, lassie, huv ye no got gloves? You'll be bloody frozen. Never mind, I'll get ye a wee brandy. A wee wan fur you and a big wan fur me. How does that sound?

That sounds great, Dad.

Aye, he says. Top o the pops, darlin. Top o the pops.

Elaine and Tony managed to talk me into coming. End of term. Big deal. Holidaytime for them, hassletime for me. Tonight I'll go home on the train with my head burling with the booze, and my pockets full of lists of unaccomplished tasks.

Elaine and Nick are all over each other, it would make you sick. He has asked her to go with him to America after graduation. She says that she hasn't decided, but she'll go. I will probably never see her again, never see any of them again. Who will I see, when I'm anchored down in Saltcoats again?

Tony and Sean bring the drinks through the crowd of students, let-loose office types, and couples who will only stay for one before they go on to somewhere more intimate.

Sean's holding the pints aloft.

Hey, Lizzie, it's bloody mental in here, isn't it?

I can't drink beer. I've tried but it made me ill. Tony hands me a vodka and tonic.

Here you are, Mrs Woman. A nice sedate wee voddie.

Shut up, Tony. It's time you found something else to slag me for. We've had this for three years now. It's getting monotonous.

He pretends to hide behind Sean.

Lizzie, he says, there's plenty I could slag you about, but I want to keep my balls.

Why? I say. You never use them.

Sean pushes Tony towards me and puts his arms round us.

C'mon you two, it's nearly Christmas. Sing a carol, grab some mistletoe, giez a kiss. Right everybody. *Away in a manger* . . . Altogether now, *O come all ye faithful* . . . What a shower of miserable bastards.

I say, Sean, I've got Randy Travis singing 'Jingle Bell Rock' in the house, if you want a loan of it.

Tony says, Randy fucking Travis? I bet you've got Pat Boone as well, and Bing Crosby.

Sean is determined to party. He holds an imaginary mike and proceeds to murder a Christmas medley. He sounds like a bad Elvis impersonator.

One of the barmaids comes round to our side.

Right big yin, she says. That's enough. There's no singing in this bar. Do you hear me?

Sean grabs her round the waist and attempts a twirl.

Aw, missus. It's Christmas. Let's have a dance. Giez a kiss.

She untangles herself and glowers up at him.

I'll dance you right out that door if I have any more of your carry-on. Now behave yourself, or you're out.

Disconsolate, Sean takes a swig of his pint.

These people are no fun. I'm going to phone Valerie. Valerie loves me. Valerie'll dance with me. I'm going to phone her.

He shambles off in the direction of the phone.

Tony laughs, I'm sure Valerie'll be delighted to hear from him. She's been waiting at his place all night. He's been in here since two o'clock, and he's well pissed. She'll probably tell him to fuck off, and he'll come back and sob all over us.

But Sean isn't sobbing, he's wearing a stupid-looking grin.

He says, I love that woman. She says I'm a big drunken idiot and I've to get in a taxi and come home. I love her.

Tony says, Aye, Sean, we know. Get your jacket and I'll get you a taxi. Lizzie, I'm going to go outside with him and make sure he gets off okay.

They leave, Sean waving at us all.

Merry Christmas everybody.

I'm left to my own devices. I could talk to umpteen people but I don't, I watch the door, wait for Tony to come back. Funny, I feel like an outsider yet none of them treats me like one. It's just that, after nights like this, I go back to another life, an alien life that they wouldn't understand.

I watch Lynne waylay Tony near the door. I wonder what happened to the lecturer? She's had her eye on Tony for a while anyway.

I have always excluded myself from the pairings-off

and couplings that take place after nights like these. I have had chances; even if the hours of darkness are forbidden, there could always be time for copulation before the curfew if I wanted to take it. I don't. I can't. I can't allow my needs or the needs of some other to intrude. It's time I went home.

Carrie is looking furtive. Every year we go through this.

Carrie, have you been sneaking about upstairs?

No, she says. I don't know what you mean.

Since they realised the non-existence of Santa, I've had to be more and more inventive in my choice of hiding places.

I say, You're wasting your time anyway, everything is round at your Auntie Bernie's. You shouldn't do that, Carrie. What if David sees you? You know he still believes in Santa.

Huh, she says. No, he doesn't. He only kids on he does, because you want him to. He knows fine it's you and my dad. You're daft, Mum.

Oh, I see. Thank you very much. Take after your father, do you? I'm daft, and the rest of you are all helluva clever, I suppose?

She sidles up beside me, knowing it's the wrong time of year to antagonise her mother.

No, she says, I didn't mean that kind of daft. Don't get your knickers in a twist. Do you want me to help you today? I'm staying in anyway. I could stick the stamps on all those Christmas cards, and then go and post them for you.

Okay, I say, on you go.

I go upstairs and leave her to it. After a minute or two, she shouts up, Yuk, Mum. I can't do this any more, it tastes rotten.

I trail back downstairs again. She's sitting cross-legged on the floor, surrounded by piles of envelopes.

Carrie, I didn't think that you were going to lick them all.

She says. That's what you do with stamps, Mum, you lick them.

Not if you have a big pile, you don't. You use a wee wet sponge. Come into the kitchen and I'll get you one.

Oh, she says, that's clever.

Equipped with the right tools for the job, she's quiet for another twenty minutes. Then she appears at the door with her coat on.

I'm going round to the post box with these. When I come back we can put the tree up; we really need to get organised, you know.

She comes back with David in tow.

Mum, tell him. He says he's helping as well. Tell him he's not. He's a wee pest. He'll just annoy us.

I really must get round to sending my CV to the SFA. Even if I never get a degree, I'm fully qualified for a job as a referee. Controlling a squad of big hairy-arsed guys would be a doddle after life chez Burns.

Carrie, cut it out. Of course David can help; it's his house too. Now, both of you, go and get the box with the decorations. No. Wait a minute. Where's Lisa? Maybe we should wait for her to get back.

David says, Aw, Mum, she won't want to help. She's down at Kirsten's; she won't care. She's too big anyway. Aw, please, let me get the box.

No. I'm going to phone her. If she doesn't want to help, that's fine, but I'm going to ask her anyway.

Lisa answers, No. Let those two do it. I'm staying at Kirsten's for my tea. I'll see you later. Bye, Mum.

Okay, you two. Go and get the box. It's just us.

They scrabble about in the hall cupboard for a while and emerge with the box full of coloured balls, Woolworths ornaments, and yards of tinsel.

Wait, Carrie says. The tape, we can't do it without the tape.

She rummages in the drawer, while I stand hoping that she won't find it. The tape. Oh God, the tape. 'Twenty Christmas Greats'. She's found it. Every year it's the same:

'Another Rock and Roll Christmas'.

Mum, tell him. Don't put that snowman on there. . . . Numpty.

'Merry Christmas Everybody'.

Give me that. You're a big pig. I'm putting the tinsel on. MUM.

'I Wish it Could be Christmas Every Day'.

There's too many balls at the bottom . . . Stupid. MUM.

'Lonely this Christmas'.

Give me that fairy. I'm putting the fairy on. MUM.

Carrie wins. Smirking at David, she carefully sets the fairy on top of the tree. I switch on the lights, and we stand back to admire. Aw. Look.

David is rolling around on the floor.

Ha ha. That fairy looks pissed.

David!

Well, she does. Look. She's all squinty. Oh ha ha.

He's right. Between her lopsided halo, her brassy-blonde hair, and her precarious stance, she looks like she's had a bloody good night on the bevy.

We collapse on the settee.

Oh ha ha . . . she's steamin.

Oh, maybe she was out with your father.

No, my grandpa. Ha ha.

Eventually, I straighten all four of us up.

I ask, What do you want for your tea?

Burgers, Carrie says, on rolls, with onions, and tomato sauce. It's Saturday; we don't need to eat real stuff.

And cakes, David says. And can we have it in here and watch the telly?

When they're parked in front of the TV with the food, I can think. Think what? Think. Will I take the easy way out, and get whisky and a cardigan for my dad, and perfume and a cardigan for Colin's mum? Think, Who bloody cares?

I wonder if Tony went off with Lynne? He usually goes for barefaced beauties, in long floral garments and granny specs. Lynne isn't his type. Lynne's everyone's type. She's probably a fantastic fuck.

What is a fantastic fuck? I mean, what would make Eddie say that I looked like a fantastic fuck? I wouldn't take him if I won him in a raffle, but I'm curious to know what he meant. What did he see? Oh, for Christ's sake, he was drunk, drunk enough to go with his granny. He didn't see anything: he's just a randy, drunken bastard.

I wonder if Tony's a fantastic fuck?

Some guy on the telly is roaring around on a motor bike. Handsome guy, lovely firm thighs. I wonder what Colin's doing? Standing in some pub in Inverness, likely. It's more of a relief than anything else when he works at the weekend.

I want to miss him. I want it to be so good that he can't bear to stay away. I want to be held and kissed when I'm on my feet, fully clothed. I want to be slowly undressed and caressed. I want to be a fantastic fuck.

For Christ's sake, woman, go and scrub something.

SIX

Christmas Eve. I am tired, and I am premenstrual.

Colin's mother does not believe in premenstrual syndrome.

Och, they never had that in my day. You're just crabbit.

We've brought her presents down. She's going to their Marjorie's tomorrow. Their Marjorie has a lovely home and she keeps it spotless. Their Marjorie would never dye her hair. Their Marjorie doesn't wear make-up. Their Marjorie's husband is a perfect gentleman. He would need to be, I can't see any man coming over all macho with their Marjorie.

I want to go to bed, alone, for a week. It could be worse. I could be pregnant. On her fortieth birthday, someone gave Bernie a mug that had I'D RATHER BE FORTY THAN PREGNANT written on it.

May hands me a carrier bag full of parcels.

She says, I just got the usual: pyjamas for the wean, and nighties for the girls. There's a couple of wee things in there for yourselves, just wee things though, I don't have the money.

I wonder what their Majorie and her perfect man will get? I'll lay odds it won't be 'just wee things'.

Colin says, Mother, you know that you don't need to bother about us.

I smile and nod in agreement. She has never bothered with me. I'm just 'her our Colin married'.

Right then, Mother, he says. We'll need to get up the road, the babysitter's going to the dancing.

I say, Yes, and I've got such a lot to do. God knows when I'll get the kids to go to sleep.

Oh well, she says, I'm sure Colin will give you a good hand.

The only thing Colin will give me is a hard time, along the lines of, Why is the house such a tip? and, Why don't I get myself organised?

We say our goodbyes, and as we're walking up the path, Colin says, Would you mind catching the bus on your own? I'm going to nip into the pub, see if Wullie's in. We need to arrange the Ne'erday darts match.

You know, I go through life thinking, I don't believe he just said that.

I say, Yes, Colin, I would mind. I would mind very much. It's Christmas Eve, and our kids are waiting at home for us. I just can't believe that you would want to piss off to the pub tonight.

As usual, when I argue, he blusters.

What the hell's up with you? I'm not going to be there all night; I'll only be half an hour or so.

Well then, Colin, if you are only going to be half an hour I'll come with you. We can both go, for half an hour.

He says, And what about that wee lassie?

She isn't going out till about nine. It's only quarter to eight.

His usual get-out clause – 'you've the weans to see to' – not having worked, he has no option but to give in gracefully. Well, actually, not gracefully; his face is tripping him, but he gives in.

The lounge bar of the Crennan Arms is almost empty. There are only two or three older couples in; the ones without kids to run after. I hate this place. In Glasgow I drink in pubs that are just pubs; here we have lounges for all the dressed-up, taken-out-for-the-night wee wifies.

Colin says, What do you want to drink?

Something innocuous, I say, my head's splitting.

He stands there, looking at me. He doesn't say anything, he just looks.

What? What is it? What's wrong?

He looks like he would like to boot me up and down this place. God knows what I've done this time. Maybe I don't need to do anything any more. Maybe he's developed some kind of seasonal disorder.

He says, If I knew what that meant, it would help.

Oh. I'm sorry. I meant something harmless, non-alcoholic. A Coke.

He gets the drinks, and we sit down, miles apart. After a while he stands up and says, I'm away through to the bar to see if Wullie's in.

Although deep down I know that I shouldn't have to apologise for extending my vocabulary, I say, Colin, I'm sorry.

Forget it, he says. I suppose I should be used to it.

He walks away, and I sit there feeling … I don't know what I'm feeling. I don't even know what I should be feeling. Christ, it was only a word. If it had been the other way round, and he had said something I didn't understand, I would have asked, said, What does that mean? I wouldn't have made him feel like he'd just crawled out from under something. Merry Christmas, Lizzie.

He comes back and picks up our empty glasses.

He says, I'm having another pint. What about you, are you still on the harmless stuff?

No, I say. Get me a vodka.

Bobby and Jean Thompson come in and sit at our table. Jean and I used to meet at the school gates every morning. Bobby plays darts with Colin.

Bobby says, You two managed to escape as well, eh?

Aye. We'll need to get back soon, though.

We're the same, Jean says. My mother's taken our two for a wee while to give us a break. It was Bobby that wanted to come out. I could have been doing with just getting on with things. Anyway, how are you getting on? Are you still doing that course thing up in Glasgow?

Aye. This is my final year. My exams start in April.

She says, What will you do then? Will you get a job?

I say, I'm not sure. I'm concentrating on the exams, I can't think about it till they're finished.

Well, she says. I'm sure I wouldn't want to go through all that bother unless I knew there was something worthwhile at the end of it. You would have been just as well getting a job when the wee one started school. I don't know how you can be bothered anyway; all that stuff would bore me. Still, I suppose it got you out of the house.

I don't believe she just said that. There, I'm doing it again. Sweeping the fucking streets would have got me out of the house. I look at Jean, sitting there, so bloody smug in her wee skirt with the kick pleats, and her nice lambswool jumper, handwashed in Dreft. Is she really happier than I am? What does she think about before she falls asleep at night?

Bobby smirks at Colin.

Aye. This education lark's okay if there's a good job at the end of it, but the young ones are finding it hard enough these days. Still, never mind, hen. Maybe Frank's wife'll get you a wee job in Tesco, next to her. You could be the only checkout lassie in Saltcoats wi a diploma or whatever it is you'll end up wi. What do you think, big man? I hear the money's no bad in there.

Colin looks at me. That look that makes me want to run a mile.

He says, It'll no matter, Bobby. If she goes on the way she's going, it'll be the big hoose she'll end up in.

The 'big hoose' is the mental hospital in Ayr, or near Ayr. I'm not really sure of its exact location. It doesn't matter; I'll find it when the time comes. Yup. Another thirteen years of this, and there'll be no need for a strait-jacket. I'll run headlong into madness. I could book my padded cell right now.

I excuse myself and head for the door with the wee woman on it.

Pink walls, peach paintwork and a machine filled with fake fragrances. I'm used to condom machines. Liquorice and Pina Colada flavours. Elaine: *I think I'll go for the Penis Collapso the night.* I'm used to graffiti. *I want to screw Craig Mathieson. Don't worry dearie. He'll get round to you.*

The big hoose. Bastard. I wonder if he knows what Eclectic means? Or Cataclysmic, or Oligarchic, or Metaphysic, or Phallocentric? Yes, that's a good one for a big prick. What about Audacious? I have the audacity to say words like Innocuous in the lounge bar of the Crennan Arms, where decent folk might hear me. Where did I put my axe?

Say your name is Lizzie Borden. Show him your axe.

I found the poem – 'Instructions to the Double'.

I look in the mirror. Hey, you with the boring bob. Get a haircut. Get a life.

I WANT TO GO HOME.

Walk back out there, towards the light reflected on Bobby's bald patch. There's a drink on the table for me. I don't want it.

I say, Colin, we need to go.

Aye, right, he says. After this one.

They are talking but their voices seem a long way away. I take a sip of the drink. I feel something like dread, like nerves before an exam. My heart's racing. My hands are shaking. I have to put the glass down. What are they saying?

Overtime ... computer for Mark ... good game ... Petite kitchen for wee Kate . . . darts match . . . mother's this year . . . what do you think? Liz Liz Liz.

I can't breathe. I have to get out of here. I have to go home.

Colin, I'm leaving. Bye, Jean . . . Bobby.

Outside, I lean against the wall. Try to breathe . . . Relax . . . Relax . . . Relax. I'm going to die. I'm going to die outside a pub, on Christmas Eve. The kids. Need the kids.

Colin comes out. He's shouting. Don't shout.

What the hell was that performance for? What the bloody hell do you think you're playing at? I'll never be able to face those folk again.

I say, Colin, I don't feel well.

That nonsense again. My mother told you, it's all in

your head. That's no excuse for cutting folk like that. Are they not good enough for you? Prefer your bloody smart pals, is that it? Christ Almighty. I'm warning you. I'm not taking much more of this. Who the hell do you think you are? You're no right in the heid, you.

Colin, I'm ill. Please. Just take me home.

He doesn't move, and so I turn and run down the hill to the taxi rank at the station. I look back, he's gone. He's gone back to face those folk. I don't care, just let me get home. Let me get home to my children. Just don't let me die on a dark Saltcoats street on Christmas Eve. Just don't let me die.

I begin to feel better as soon as the taxi stops at my gate. The fear's gone. Just one more deep breath before the door opens and Lisa's standing there.

Mum, you're all white. What's the matter with you? Where's Dad?

I say, I'm fine, I've just got a bit of a headache. Your dad's away for a pint. I came back to let Jill away.

The other two don't even acknowledge me, they're watching television.

Jill says, You should have gone with him, I'm not in a hurry. The night doesn't really start till after eleven. I've put their presents under the tree. I had to watch this boy like a hawk; he would have had the paper ripped off.

I give Jill her gifts from us, and I get the kids up to do the same.

Oh, she says, I'll need to go now, or I'll greet and ruin my make-up. Thanks very much. I'll see you all next week, but give me a ring if you need me before then. Bye. Merry Christmas.

Bye Jill. Merry Christmas. Don't get too drunk.

Bye Jill. Merry Christmas. Hope you get a lumber.

Bye. Merry Christmas. Bye.

The kids go back to the telly, and I dial Bernie's number.

Hello, Bernie? It's me. He's in the pub, and I don't know when he'll be back. He probably won't be in a fit state to come round for the kids' things.

That's okay, she says, we'll bring them round after Midnight Mass. What's he doing in the pub? He should be there with you and the weans. Are you okay? What's happened?

I say, We were in the Crennan. He wanted to go in for half an hour, on the way back from his mother's. I had this, I don't know, some kind of panic, anxiety thing. I felt absolutely terrible. We were sitting with Bobby and Jean Thompson. I felt so bloody ill. Honestly, Bernie, I thought I was going to die. I ran out, just got up and left. He was raging. He wouldn't come home with me.

The bastard, she says. No wonder you're having panic attacks, you've been doing far too much, lassie. Get Lisa to make you a cup of tea, and you sit on your arse for a while. I'll be round after Mass. If he comes in and starts, just ignore him. And don't you worry; a night with the Thompsons would be enough to give anybody a panic attack. Did she have one of her handknitted frocks on?

No, I say, a wee navy skirt, and a fully-fashioned jumper.

Bernie says, She must have blitzed Moira's Separates again. Right. Get that tea, or something stronger if you feel like it. Sit down and relax. Okay? I'll see you later. Bye.

It's almost eleven when Colin finally rolls in. Lisa's still up, keeping me company. He's only had three hours tonight. A short shift.

I hate this. I hate the tension. Hate it, hate it, hate it. Taking too long to notice that I'm digging my fingernails into my palms, and clenching my teeth so hard that my jaw aches.

Hard to smile and speak and be normal, be the wife, be the mummy. Hard. There's something hard inside my chest. A concrete wall there, and if it crumbles, if I shout, if I scream or cry, and it crumbles, we'll all fall down.

He's slumped on the couch, grinning at Lisa. I wonder for the umpteenth time why it is that, when he's drunk, his features seem to drop about six inches down his face. Sober, he's okay, considered handsome by some, but when he's drunk, he looks like . . . I don't know what he looks like . . . something slack and unravelled, like the knitting that I could never finish. He looks like my knitting. He looks like fuck all.

He says, Hey, Lisa, did you know that your mother canny even bear to be out wi me? Had to run away. We're no intellectual enough, me and Mr and Mrs Thompson. You know Mrs Thompson, don't you, hen? Nice woman. No like your mum, eh? What d'ye think?

Lisa and I exchange looks that say, Humour him, and he'll fall asleep. Already she is an expert. Talk in a monotonous tone. It doesn't matter what you say, just drone on, smile a lot, and talk nicely. Then maybe he'll fall asleep. If he falls asleep, we won't have to put up with his collapsing face, and his drivelling repartee. If he falls asleep here, then he won't fall asleep in the bathroom, and they won't have to call downstairs, *Mum, get my daddy out, I'm bursting*. If he falls asleep, we will be able to get up on Christmas morning, and pretend that it never happened.

Lisa says, Dad, don't be silly, Mum just had a sore head. Why don't you lie down and rest? It's nearly Christmas. Jill's away to a disco, she had mistletoe with her, she says she's going to kiss all the boys. Sure that's funny, Dad? Have a wee rest, it'll be Christmas soon.

We watch his eyelids droop. His breathing deepens, the

start of a snore. Afraid to move. One more minute. His head jerks up.

Christmas. I've got to go round to Frank's.

He struggles up and stands, swaying. He must have gone on the shorts after I left.

You, he says, you don't care about the weans' presents. I care, I love them. You don't care about them. I care. I'll go.

I say, Colin, it's okay. Sit down. Frank and Bernie are bringing them round later.

No. I'll do it. I care about my weans.

He staggers over to me, hangs on to the back of my chair.

I care, he says. You'd rather be fucking around up in Glasgow.

He steps back, and then he's falling, falling backwards, crashing on to the Christmas tree. The tree that the kids decorated. He lies there surrounded by snowmen and tinsel. By some kind of miracle he's missed the presents that were lying under it.

Ah, to hell wi it, he says, to hell wi the lot of ye. Fucking around. Mental bitch.

David is calling downstairs.

Mum, is it morning? Mum.

Lisa says, I'll go. I'll take him in beside me. Will you be okay?

I say, I'll be fine, he's asleep now. Hurry up or the wean'll come down.

I brush her hair with my hand. My babies should have no part in all of this.

Go on, Lisa, it'll all be all right in the morning. Night-night.

I hear her talking to David on the stairs.

C'mon, son. No, it isn't morning. Do you want to come into my bed? I'll read you *The Night Before Christmas.*

I look at him, lying drunk on the floor on Christmas Eve. Maybe that's what the fear is: fear of facing it, facing him. Facing him with the words. I thought that you would love me, save me, take care of me, be with me, share with me, laugh with me, grow up with me, grow old with me. You can't, you won't, you never will. I am afraid to speak.

I turn away from him, and pour myself a very large glass of wine, sit down and wait. Drinking and waiting to feel that I can cope again.

I hear the car stopping outside, then the click of Bernie's heels on the path. I'd forgotten that they were coming. I open the door and Frank carries David's mountain bike in past me. Bernie appears behind him, carrying boxes.

She says, Hello, hen. Merry Christmas. I couldn't get Frank to wear a Santa suit. They sleeping?

They stop dead in the living room, and stare at our ghost of Christmas past, present and future lying on the floor.

Frank says, I'll straighten that tree up for you, hen, as if Colin wasn't there.

Bernie says, Come out to the motor, Lizzie, and we'll get the rest of the stuff.

I go with her, and she whispers on the path, What the hell happened? He didn't hit you, did he?

No. He just fell.

We unload the car and take the stuff into the kitchen, in case one of the kids comes down. I put the kettle on, and Bernie rifles in the fridge.

What have you got for a sandwich? I've just had Communion, I'm bloody starving.

I start to make sandwiches. I stand with the knife in my

hand, but I don't know what I'm doing. I sit down at the table.

I say, Bernie, I don't think I can cope.

She comes over and puts her arms round me.

Oh, you'll cope, hen, you shouldn't have to, but you will. Just get through tomorrow, and we'll be round on Boxing Day to cheer you up. Your dad's coming tomorrow, isn't he? Well, that'll be nice for you. Just concentrate on the weans during the day. And when they're in bed, you run yourself a nice aromatherapy bath, and have an early night. You'll cope.

We have the sandwiches and the rest of the wine. When they've gone I go straight to bed. He probably won't make it up the stairs tonight. *I* should have read that story to David.

While visions of sugarplums danced in their heads.

Christmas shouldn't be like this. Christmas is supposed to be about peace and goodwill towards men.

Families. Christmas is supposed to be about families; not one woman trying to make it good for everyone else. Christmas should be happy children and Midnight Mass and fireglow and robins.

Where is my goodwill toward men?

Nowhere. I have none. Tomorrow Rachel will have Christmas lunch in a Tuscan garden with her charming friends and her talented husband and her little daughter. I would give anything to have my mother arriving here tomorrow; to have my parents here together, with us. My dad will come alone. Nothing will be the way I want it to be. Colin will be even worse this year, and no I haven't cleaned the house or changed the curtains. And yes, I will make an arse of cooking the turkey.

I hate turkey. When I was young we all went to

Granny's, and we had chicken. A great luxury, was chicken. When I grew up and discovered that you were supposed to have turkey I felt embarrassed, but when I was wee I hadn't minded. Children never seem to mind. Mine will think they're the luckiest weans in the world because they'll have a mum and dad, and a grandpa, and presents and food, and big films on the telly.

I remember the presents. The wicker sewing basket, and the dolly with long blonde hair. I named her Mandy, after Mandy Rice-Davies, and my mother laughed all day at me calling my dolly after a prostitute. On Boxing Day I cut off all her hair with the scissors from the sewing basket.

My presents were all domestic; flashy kid-on labour-saving devices.

The washing machine that actually washed, and the Little Betty sewing machine. By rights I should have grown up a paragon of domestic virtue, but my aunties managed to turn that one on its head.

My aunties: Adele and Sonia. Funny names for Saltcoats lassies, Adele and Sonia. Destined for greater things, they were. All glamorous and sexy: Manhattan perfume, in the box that looked like a night-time skyscraper, Sobranne cigarettes, and Amami setting lotion, used only in the middle of the week because they went to the hairdresser in Ayr every Saturday afternoon. Wee Senga's salon was never good enough for Adele and Sonia.

Sonia always gave me reading and writing stuff for Christmas: books and notepads and artist's sketch-pads with funny square-ended pencils. Adele bought me a toy switchboard; not just a wee telephone, but a big red switchboard.

They both worked for the GPO, at the big exchange in Ayr. Sometimes they took me in to work with them on a

Saturday morning. We caught the early train, Adele in her astrakhan coat and her exotic winged glasses, Sonia in a leopardskin jacket and tight skirt, with a wiggle that would have put Marilyn Monroe to shame. I had to be quiet while they were working, so there was always a new book for me in Sonia's bucket bag. I would twirl round on a swivel chair, lost in *Lorna Doone* or *What Katy Did*, while they plugged in tangles of wires and talked in their special voices.

Just putting you through, caller ...

The number you require is ...

Then lunch in the tearoom, where I learned the correct way to use your cutlery, how to eat eclairs without getting cream on your face, and how to apply lipstick in a perfect Cupid's bow.

I learned a lot from Adele and Sonia. I learned that if you worked at the right job, and wore the right clothes, you would meet the right men. I also learned that if you married the right man, and you gave up your job to have four or five kids, then you would end up a Valium- or Librium-addicted housewife, or a sad alcoholic, taping your glasses up with Sellotape, and letting your dark roots grow in.

Merry Christmas, Adele and Sonia. Thank you for the gifts.

Same cheery mood, I see, Bernie says.

We're drinking Boxing Day sherry; it's a ritual. Bernie and I have many rituals: Boxing Day at my place, New Year's Day at hers – I sing 'Your Cheating Heart', and she jives with Frank to 'Runaround Sue' – sunbathing in her garden on hot days, because mine is a tangle of weeds, bikes, and footballs. We go to the pictures once a fortnight, taking it in turns to choose the film. Our rituals have remained, unchanging, through all of the other changes.

When we met, she was a wee housewife, and I was a daft wee lassie. She got a life, and I got kids and qualifications. I think she's happy, and I know I'm not. I don't know if I ever will be, but if I told her that, she would be angry.

What's up with his face, anyway? she says.

Me, Christmas, me running out on him like that, on Christmas Eve. It was murder yesterday: I forgot to take the giblets out of the bloody turkey, that really made his day. He hardly spoke to me. Merry Christmas when he opened his presents, that was about all. We kept it all very civilised for the sake of the kids and my dad, but I know what he was thinking: I hadn't cleaned the house from top to bottom, the way his mother always did. That'll be it: the saga of the dirty hoose.

Huh, she says. More like an aversion to spending a full day in the hoose, with his own family.

In spite of what she says, I know that it is all my fault. I should be able to do what other women do. I should be able to make him want to be here.

Bernie kicks off her shoes and tucks her feet under her, reaching for the sherry bottle at the same time. Frank's building a model with David, and the girls are upstairs, tunelessly screeching to music that no one else can hear; both plugged into new Walkmans. They can relax today, best behaviour is not compulsory. Colin disappeared about ten minutes ago; he must be upstairs too.

Bernie is still enraged.

That daft big bugger doesn't know how lucky he is. Why doesn't he just accept what you're doing? I mean, it's been over three years, and you've managed so well.

I say, He never will. He thinks I'm trying to make a fool out of him.

I don't know, she says. What would you do with him? I

mean, I'm really fond of Colin, you couldn't meet a nicer big fella; but you're not making a fool of him. He's making a great job of doing that all by himself.

Colin comes into the room, and Bernie raises her voice.

Well, hen, I wish I had half your guts. You can be proud of yourself and what you're going to achieve.

He lets that pass. He's too fond of Frank and Bernie to start an argument today. He hands Frank another beer. The model's finished.

Look Dad, David says. Look at my model. Uncle Frank helped me a wee bit. Look at it, Dad. Sure it's brilliant? It's a Spitfire, Dad. Look at it.

Colin glances down at the model.

That's great, son. Put your video on.

How much effort does it require to look at a stupid wee model? Would it kill him just to pay attention for once, to a child whose whole being is waiting for his company, his interest, and his praise? The man hasn't a bloody clue, and I can't bear to see that look on David's face, again.

Bernie slides down on to the floor beside the wean.

Oh my, David, that is just wonderful. Colin, come down here, and see what this boy has done. He's going to be an engineer when he grows up; I can tell. Sure you are, son? He'll make a fortune for his mammy. Won't you, darlin?

Colin ruffles David's hair.

He says, Aye. That's pretty good, wee man.

I suppose that's about the best any of us can expect.

Frank sits down next to me.

Christ, he says, my legs are sore from kneeling down there. I'll tell you something, that boy's no bother when he's got something to occupy him.

Aye, I know, I say, and somebody taking the time to do it with him.

Frank smiles. I've got all the time in the world for making models now that our two are grown up. Sometimes it's hard to see what's needed when you're in amongst it all. Then they grow up, and you wish that you could make them wee again, just so that you could get to do all the things you didn't do. Maybe that's just the way it works, hen. I must say, I'm looking forward to the day when I become a grandpa; I'll have some wee spud spoiled stupid.

I say, You'll make a wonderful grandpa, Frank, and I can't wait for the chance to call her Granny Bernie.

Bernie laughs, You'll need to find me first, and then you'll need to catch me. I'm too busy for all of that. Maybe in ten years or so. When I've calmed down.

Colin says, You'll never calm down, Bernie. You and your pal there, you'll never be sane.

Lisa and Carrie emerge from their bedroom, and claim all the attention. Frank opens his arms wide, and they squeeze in either side of him.

Hello, my flowers of the burning desert. Was Santa good to you?

Bernie and I take the bottle into the kitchen with us. She slices mushrooms, and I chop onions, and Patsy Cline sings heartache songs.

I say, Frank's good, he's a good man.

Aye, if you take him the right way, by the throat.

C'mon, you know you don't mean that.

They're all the same, she says. I love Frank, but basically they're all the same.

But you're okay, I say. You moved from checkout lassie to under manager, and he was really proud of you. He's backed you all the way.

I know, she says, but it's still only working in a shop. That's allowed, no injured pride there, it's just a wee job.

We cook, just like we've done for years. Only the menus have changed: we skin chicken breasts, crush garlic, toss pasta in aromatic sauces, where once we would have mixed frozen prawns into cocktails, grilled steaks, and defrosted Black Forest gateaux.

The meal is good. Mum, Dad, Auntie and Uncle, all delighted with the food and the wine and the weans. We have had years of this, we should have years more.

Colin, Frank, and David do the dishes. Another tradition. Lisa and Carrie make the coffee, and Bernie and I stretch out and light up. We've had plenty of stop-smoking pacts but we always come up with the same excuse: my nerves were shattered.

When we are all settled, Bernie says, Oh, Frank, I forgot to tell Lizzie and Colin what happened. You know, when we were up in Glasgow last week. Honestly, Lizzie, what a laugh. We were in Debenhams, looking for underwear for our Linda. We had already got her jewellery, but you know me, I like to make up lots of parcels. Anyway, I'm standing there, and I thought I saw you, from the back. I said to Frank, There's Lizzie, we can all go for coffee, and go back together on the train. So I walked up to this woman, that I thought was you, and I tapped her on the shoulder and I said, Right, miss, I am arresting you for shoplifting. Well, she turned round, and she was your double, except that she was absolutely caked in make-up. I'm no kidding you, I have never seen that much make-up on the one face. I thought, Oh Jesus Christ, she's been Rimmelled. I got such a fright. I stood there stuttering and apologising. I didn't know where to put my face.

Frank says, Aye, and the best of it was, two minutes earlier I thought I saw the big man here, going out of the shop. We're definitely going senile, us two.

Bernie and Frank are both sprawled out on the settee laughing; tears pouring down Bernie's cheeks.

That's funny, I say. Two of my friends spotted a woman that looked really like me, once in Edinburgh and once in Glasgow; and both of them said she was with a big tall guy. Maybe there's a couple going around impersonating us. Eh, Colin, what do you think?

He says, I think your pals are all about as bloody daft as yourself.

Merry Christmas, darling.

SEVEN

I trail downstairs in my dressing gown, hoping for five minutes' peace before David gets up. What a bloody night, filled with terrible, frightening dreams. In the first one a giant tortoise suddenly appeared: a giant male tortoise. He was outside, blocking the front gate when I tried to leave in the morning. I ran back into the house and out the back way, but he was there, down at the fence, and although in the dream it was winter, the daffodils that always grow there in the spring were in bloom. Then I was at the railway station, but he blocked the way to the platform. He appeared again, at the main gates of the University, preventing me from getting to my lectures.

The tortoise is familiar to me: we know each other well. I feel a certain tenderness towards him, I know that he doesn't want to harm me. This creature loves me, he only wants me to notice him. In the dream I was overcome with guilt because I wished that he would go away.

I woke up feeling guilty and sad. Lay there, smoking in the dark, feeling more alone than I think I've ever felt. I must have eventually drifted off again straight into another nightmare:

I come home and find my neighbour, Grace, in my kitchen. She's wearing a frilly apron and holding a cloth, and everything is clean and sparkling. She says, *Oh, you're back, are you? You should be ashamed of yourself, gallivanting away up there, and I'm left here to take care of your man.* I go into the living-room, and see Colin sitting with his back to me. Grace follows and stands behind me, and I'm trapped between them. Colin slowly rises from the chair; he's wearing old-fashioned striped pyjamas and a dressing gown. His movements are feeble and weak. He turns and stumbles towards me, holding out his skeletal hand for me to take, and his face is a skull. Grace disappears, and I'm alone with him. That's when I woke up again, with my heart racing, and tears on my cheeks.

Time at home. Time to study, time to finish my long-overdue essay on the Brontës, time to plot and pin up the study plan, time to figure out what the hell I'm doing.

What am I doing? I'm staring out of the window, that's what I'm doing.

The view is boring; there are a few cows in the field, and sometimes there are sheep and horses. I have the best of both worlds, you see. I'm right next to the countryside, but if I stand up, hang out of the window and twist my neck, I can see the sea. Cars come up here to turn in the cul-de-sac, but cars are almost as boring as cows. School children pass, morning and afternoon, but they represent responsibility, also boring. School cleaners hurry past in the early morning and late afternoon, but they're the most boring of all. They are invariably drab, they are not colourfully dressed or glamorous, and I've given up wishing that one day one of them would shout, Fuck the floor polisher! mount one of the horses and go galloping off into the sunset. They do damn all to alleviate my boredom.

Jill had to go to the dentist, that's why I'm here, spending time at home. They give her this knockout jab, and it leaves her like a wee rag dolly, she says. I hope she'll be all right for tomorrow, I have to take this essay up to Jim.

Write the bloody thing. My essays used to be 'golden loaves'. Now they're more like biscuits, flat and boring. Note the use of culinary metaphors. Why can't I just write essays, like every other bugger? My approach to essay writing is similar to my approach to housework – procrastinate, procrastinate, procrastinate. Find another book, take some more notes, then piss about for days, smoking, drinking coffee, and staring out of this window.

Professor Sloan was right: I'll never get a degree. I shouldn't be there if I can't do the work. I'm a fraud. All this time, I've been running away from my responsibilities, kidding on that I'm a student. I've fooled everyone. *Shakespeare's tragic women are victims, viragoes or whores. Ulysses. Villette. Sons and Lovers.* Eliot. Pound. Plath. I talk a good game. I'll be found out when my name fails to appear on the roll of triumph in College Square.

Elisabeth Mary Burns. MA Fuck all.

Dishonoured.

Maybe I should get up and load the machine, change Lisa's sheets. I was used to sorting out three wee piles of pants and vests and socks. Now there are bras and pre-soaked knickers and blood-stained sheets tumbling around with my children's washing. The girl whose laundry has moved into my pile rarely smiles, and her conversation is monosyllabic: *So? Well? Godsake!*

I have to finish this, I have to. The thought of not getting the work done can bring on the panic attacks. Jim doesn't know about them, none of them does. I told Bernie, and she bought me a relaxation tape for my Walkman. It has 'Deep Relaxation' on one side, and 'Tranquillity' on the other. The woman's voice gets on my nerves: *You are filled with inner peace.*

You are at peace ... You are at peace ... You are at peace.

Am I hell. I am bloody terrified.

It's Bernie's day off today. I think I'll give her a ring.

Hi, Bernie.

Hello. How come you're not at Uni?

Oh, Jill had to go to the dentist. I'm supposed to be writing an essay but my head's full of mince.

Well, take a break. Come round, I'll stick the kettle on.

When I get there, Bernie's drawings are scattered across the table. Bernie, I shouldn't be disturbing you.

Och, she says, I was only sorting them out. Here, I was just looking at this one when you phoned.

She hands me the sketch. Lisa, looking up, with her chin cupped in her hands, and just a wee smile. Lisa.

Bernie says, It only seems like yesterday that you brought her home from the hospital. And remember when she was sitting up in her big pram, and she had such a dirty laugh? Folk used to turn to see where it was coming from, and there was this wee thing, all dolled up in pink, haw-hawing away.

Yes, I remember. She isn't laughing much these days.

She says, Och, that's just her age. Boys seem to just lie about in the dark a lot, and only come out to eat you out of house and home, but lassies have it hard. It'll pass, you'll see.

Oh aye, Bernie, it'll pass, and then it'll be Carrie's turn. I coped with the terrible twos, but I don't know if I can cope with the terrible teens.

You'll cope, she says, just like the rest of us. Now, go and make the coffee, while I clear this lot away.

We sit at the table with the mugs and the biscuit tin. If I put biscuits in a tin, they're all gone by bedtime. I hide them, under the sink, and in the oven. Once, I forgot, and switched it on; melted all the KitKats.

She says, Have you recovered from Christmas yet?

Are you kidding? I don't think I'll ever recover.

I know, she says. You had a helluva time, hen. I said to Frank when we got back on Boxing Night, It just isn't fair, what he's doing to that lassie. Christmas is always a strain, though. I mean, look at us: our two came home on Christmas Eve, and they were away just after dinner on Christmas Day. He was mad, because I ended up in tears. But what can you do? You think that everybody in the bloody country is doing the happy families bit, but they're not. I'm getting to be that I could see it all far enough.

I say, Well, it's over now. I'm trying to concentrate on studying for my finals; if I could just get myself organised I'd be fine.

I'm here if you need me, she says. I love having the weans, so does Frank, especially that David, he's a hoot, so he is.

I say, That's not all he is, he's a wee bugger.

No, he isn't. David's a good boy. They're three lovely weans. You just need a bit more help with them, that's all. You should have a look in the *Ardrossan and Saltcoats Herald*; see if Mary Poppins is available for the next three months. If she's not advertising, Auntie Bernadette will come round with her umbrella and her carpetbag.

Oh, Bernie, I say. We're as bloody daft as each other.

I know. Great, in't it?

I get home just before David bursts in with his shirt hanging out, his tie loosened, and his shoelaces undone.

I say, I take it you had gym?

Jim who? he says.

He rifles in his schoolbag, and brings out a letter.

That's from the school dentist, Mum.

David has an abscess, and will have to take a course of anti-biotics before his treatment next week. He will have to be collected from school at two pm on Wednesday 22, as he will be drowsy after his treatment.

More time at home.

Right, I say, I'll get your prescription tomorrow, and I'll collect you next Wednesday.

He places another letter on the table, and backs away, towards the door.

I'm going up to get changed, he says.

No cartoons, no wild whoops or karate kicks on the way upstairs: just the sound of a boy beating a hasty retreat. I sit down with the letter. I hardly need to open it, they're all the same: *David is inattentive. David is disobedient. David is disruptive.* I could paper the back porch with them. Keep waiting for the one that says, *David is bored bloody rigid.* I open the letter.

David, get down here. Now.

He comes down a lot slower than he went up. I grab him by the shoulders.

What the hell were you doing up on the school roof?

Getting the ball, he says.

Whose ball?

Stuart's ball.

If it was Stuart's ball, why did you go up on the roof to get it?

Oh, Mum, because it was me that kicked it up there.

Gripping his arms, shaking him, hard.

You could have been killed, you stupid, stupid boy. You could have fallen and you would be dead. Are you listening to me?

Seeing the fear flit across his face because his mother, the woman who preaches tolerance and non-violent protest, is shaking the bloody life out of him. Pulling him close and feeling his wee thin body. Seeing him lying bloody and broken on the playground.

He's rubbing tears away with his fist. He hardly ever cries.

David, don't you ever do anything like that again. You don't need to climb up things and jump off things all the bloody time. Why can't you just play, like any other wean?

I'm sorry, Mum. I was okay. I'm sorry.

Carrie marches in. She pushes David out of her way.

Do you know what he did? Do you know?

Yes, Carrie.

I need a coffee. A drink would be even better, but I won't add alcoholic to Colin's list of insults. Carrie stands over David, shouting.

You are mental, she says. You're loopy, you shouldn't be at my school, you should be at the special school. You are definitely loopy.

Carrie, that is enough, I say.

But Mum, she says, it was horrible. I was round in the big playground, and Lorna Smith's wee sister and some other wee girls came round and said, Come and see what your wee brother's doing, and we went round, and he was up there, on the roof, dancing about like a loony and shouting down to his pals. Then he started wobbling about at the edge, kidding on he was going to fall, and I felt sick. And then the jannie climbed up and got him down. And when we were back in the class I started crying, and everybody was looking at me, and Miss McKee had to take me to the medical room. She phoned here, but nobody was in. If he's not mental, then he's bad, he's really bad, Mum.

I send David up to his room, and I pour juice, and retrieve the biscuits from under the sink. Bang goes that hiding place. I sit Carrie down at the table, pour my coffee, and sit down next to her.

Carrie, listen to me. He is not mental, and he is not bad. I know it must have been frightening for you, and what he did was very stupid and very wrong, but he isn't bad. He just has too much energy and not enough fear, that's all. Calling him names isn't going to help.

She says, You always stick up for him. You weren't there, you weren't crying, everybody wasn't looking at you. I hate him, and I hate you. I want my dad to come home, he would make him behave.

She runs out of the room, and I sit for a minute before I think to check that she isn't upstairs, strangling him. I listen. She's in her own room, bawling and kicking the wall. I sit on the stairs.

Lisa comes in the front door.

Why are you here? Where's Jill? What's she making all that racket for? Have we got any Feminax? My stomach's killing me. When's tea?

I say, Lisa, could you wait, just a minute?

Carrie's standing behind me, sniffing and holding out a letter.

The school nurse says I've got to go to the chiropodist.

I've got verrucas. I told you my foot was sore. You didn't listen, you never listen.

Lisa barges past.

I hate this house. Godsake!

Puberty. Periods. Dental decay. Suicidal tendencies. Sibling rivalry. Neglect. Fungal infections.

Time at home.

I hate Saturdays. The kids are driving me mental.

Mum, tell him.

Mum, it wasn't me, it was her.

I hate her.

I hate you, ya wee pig.

Mum, he's hitting me.

Mum.

Nowhere to go. Nothing to do. Everybody else is otherwise engaged: going out, going shopping, and going to their mother's. I'm going nowhere. Stuck up here, while he's down there with the boys in the bar. The troops, he calls them. I bet the troops would like to put me up against a wall and shoot me, no blindfold. Grey, suffocating Saturday; I think I'd prefer execution.

The phone rings, I bet it's for Lisa. It's Rachel.

Hi, Rachel. How are you?

I'm fine; it's you I'm worried about. Your tutor is worried about you too. He called me yesterday to ask about you.

I'm fine, Rachel. I don't know what Jim's on about. Anyway, how's your mother?

She's fine. We found her a very good place, and she's as happy there as she would be anywhere. The important thing is that she's well cared for, and that is such a load off my mind. Now, about you. When can you come up and see me? How about Monday lunchtime?

Okay. Monday lunchtime, but I'm fine.

Yes, Lizzie, you're fine. I'll see you Monday. Bye.

Well. Talk of the place again, Lizzie. I wonder what kind of Saturdays Rachel has? Busy, probably. I bet her husband's there. Tonight they'll have dinner, maybe have friends round, something civilised.

David comes in, holding his face.

Mum, my tooth's sore.

I give him his medicine, and heat up some soup for his tea. Carrie declares that she isn't hungry and why can't she have soup? Lisa used to eat whatever was put in front of her, but nowadays my cooking can't compare with Kirsten's and Mandy's mothers'. They argue continually at the table, and eventually I leave them to it. I go into the living room and sit in front of the TV, not watching, just staring at the bloody thing, while I yearn for pasta and pavlova and adult company.

They follow me through.

Can we watch the video now?

Yes. Put it on.

I close the blinds, and they settle down in front of *Bigfoot and the Hendersons*. I wonder when my own Bigfoot will come rolling home?

Ten o'clock, and I hear the taxi stopping outside. The tension building up inside me. Stomach-churning tension. Why? He's never violent. If I could bring myself to do what I used to do, and talk nice to him, and feed him, he would be okay. No, he was never okay. When I was expecting Lisa, he was just the same. Strolling in, criticisms at the ready: *You canny even make a decent dinner. You're no fit to have my wean.*

Now I have three of his weans.

He stands, swaying in front of me.

Is there any chance of a meal in this place? I mean, I'm the one that's bringing in the money, but I canny even get something to eat.

I say, Well, next time, just you give me a call, and I'll put on my wee twirly skirt and my roller skates, and whizz it down to you on a silver tray.

He says, You're so smart, so clever. Love putting me down, don't you? C'mere, lassies. What do you think of your smart mother?

Lisa and Carrie position themselves next to me.

I see, he says, it's like that, is it? You've even managed to turn *them* against me.

They look at me, and I know that it's up to me. It's up to me to make it all right. I can't have them standing beside their mother, fearful of their own father. This isn't the way things were meant to be.

I say, You two go on up to bed, I'll make your dad something to eat. Go on, I'll come up in a wee while.

They go, and I go into the kitchen, put a shepherd's pie in the microwave. It won't matter what I give him, he'll probably fall asleep before it's ready. He just needs to know that I'm in here, doing my job.

I hear David in the living-room.

It's my sore tooth again, Dad.

I go in, and Colin turns on me.

What's the matter with this boy's teeth?

I start to say, The school dentist said ...

He roars, What have I told you about the school dentist? Yer own wean suffers because you canny be bothered to take him to a decent dentist.

The girls are back downstairs, and the three of them are standing, scared, between us. Why does he have to do this? I grab David and push the girls towards the door.

I say, You're wrong. You are so bloody wrong. My own wean only suffers when his drunken bastard of a father comes home.

I take them all up to bed, and I give David his medicine, and I tell them that it will all be all right. I'll make it all right.

I wake up late the next morning. There's no sign of him, he must have slept in the chair all night. I can hear the TV blaring, David's cartoons.

Colin comes in carrying a tray with two mugs of coffee. He never usually bothers with peace-offerings.

He says, I've given them their breakfast, they're watching the telly.

I push myself up against the pillows, and take the coffee. This feels embarrassing somehow, too intimate. You can screw when you're not in love, but it's difficult to keep doing nice things for each other.

He says, I'll pack my bag, I'm going to catch an earlier train. I've been thinking. This isn't working. I'm going to stay at my mother's at the weekends.

I say, Colin, you don't need to do that.

Aye, I do. You don't want me here. I've tried, Liz. All this university stuff, I just can't get my head round it. You and the weans have made your own life, without me.

I say, That's because we've had to, Colin. You don't want to be with us. You want to be with the boys in the pub. We never do anything as a family, you don't want to spend any time with us.

He says, When we got married, I thought that we had made a deal: I would work and earn the money, and you would take care of the house and the kids. You wanted it too, Liz, you wanted weans. You changed, always reading bloody books; books that told you how much you should hate men, especially me.

I say, I don't hate you. But you make it bloody impossible to love you. Of course I changed. Did you think that I would stay eighteen for ever? I thought that we would grow up and change together, other couples do.

He gets up, and walks round the bed, stands staring out of the window with his back to me.

I won't change now, I'll never change. Anyway, it's too late, there's nothing left. We're not exactly red-hot lovers, are we?

I say, Do you still love me?

Aye, he says, I do, I've never loved anybody else, but that's not enough, is it?

I can't just lie here while this conversation's going on. I jump up and put on a dressing gown. I should get dressed. If he means this, if this is it, then I can't just lie here wearing a Mickey Mouse t-shirt.

I say, What about the weans? What will we tell them?

He says, I don't think it'll bother them that much. They're used to me being away, they're used to you and Bernie, and that wee lassie. I'll come down at the weekends and see them. It won't be that different.

Of course it will be different. They'll be the children of a broken home. How different do you want it to be? It won't be that different? That's your best one yet, Colin. How fucking stupid can you get?

That look again.

There's no need for talk like that, he says.

What? You've just told me that you're not happy in this marriage, this house, and this family. You've just told me that you don't want to come home any more. And you think that there's no need for talk like that? Send for the vocabulary police.

There you go again, you and your smart talk. You and your education, and your daft ideas. What has any of that got to do wi me and the weans? You think that going about talking a load of pish like that makes you better than me. That's what started it, that's what turned you into somebody I didn't even know. When I met you, you were making brassieres in a factory in Paisley; an ordinary lassie wi an ordinary job. And you wanted an ordinary life, wi a man and weans and a nice house.

I say, We could have done it together, you and me and the weans. You could have supported me, Colin.

Supported you? I've supported this family for years. You could have got a wee job, helped out, like other women. I've to go out and knock my melt in to keep you in denim jackets and school bags. I've kept my side of the deal, you're in the wrong and you know it.

I want to get dressed but if I take off this t-shirt I'll be naked. I've lived with this man for thirteen years, he's watched me giving birth, for Christ's sake, and now I can't even put my knickers on in front of him. I would kill for another coffee and a cigarette.

I say, I'm going downstairs. I want a fag and a coffee. There's no sense in going on with this conversation. We're getting nowhere.

Oh aye, he says. Walk away, you're good at that.

You sanctimonious big bastard. Walk away? That's all you've ever done. Every bloody weekend since I married you. You've done nothing but walk away from those children and me. The pub, the boozer, the boys, the troops. Oh aye, the troops. Only someone as bloody stupid as you would call a lot of fucking drunken wasters 'the troops'. Have they all got wee green berets and toy rifles? Is that what you are, Colin, a frustrated sergeant major? Pissing off with the troops every time I refuse to obey orders? You can't put all the blame on me. Where were you every time you were needed? Where were you when David went missing? Where were you when Carrie fell off her bike and broke her wrist? Where were you when they had measles and chickenpox and mumps? I was here. You were in the pub with the troops. No days at the shore, no Daddy at the birthday parties. Oh aye, you were a provider, but don't kid yourself that you were ever a husband and father: that takes a helluva lot more than five shifts and double time on a Sunday.

He brings out the holdall from the side of the wardrobe, starts packing the jeans and shirts and socks and boxer shorts that I washed yesterday.

He says, Who are you kidding? What was there for me to come home for? You know, when I get back on a Friday I head down to Central for the train home. I see guys going into that shop, buying sexy underwear for their wives. I think, What's the use? She wouldn't wear it; women's libbers don't wear stuff like that. You'd rather take a book to bed, wouldn't you, Liz?

My side of the deal: clean claes, hot dinners, and hot sex. I've had enough of this.

Colin, do whatever you want, stay away or come home. But I won't tolerate another drunken weekend. If you come back here, then you stay sober. You stay with us, and you stay sober.

He lifts the holdall and his jacket.

He says, I'm not one of those poofs you're in the habit of mixing with these days. If I want to go for a few pints, I will. I'll be back at the weekend but I'll be staying at my mother's, I'll see the weans there.

Thirteen years. Thirteen years and he can arrange for his children to visit him. Thirteen years and he can just walk away with a bag full of clean washing.

He goes downstairs. I stay where I am. Where am I? Sitting on our bed, in our bedroom, in our house.

I have to go down there.

He's sitting on the settee with Lisa. The other two are standing facing him. They turn round when I come in.

Carrie says, Why can't my dad stay here when he comes back?

I don't know what he's said to them. We should have rehearsed this.

He says, It's okay, hen. I told you. I need to stay at Nana's when I come back. Your mum'll bring you down there on Saturday.

I want to ask him how he can see them on a Saturday. What about the troops? Will there be insurrection in the ranks? And what will we do on their birthdays? What will we do on our anniversary? Who'll bring them to my graduation?

Oh God.

He stands, bends down to kiss them.

Now you behave for your mum. I'll see you on Saturday.

I walk with him to the door.

He says, I'll phone you to arrange about Saturday. We'll need to talk about things.

How are we supposed to do this? What's the protocol? Do we shake hands? Kiss for the last time? He opens the door, and the cold rushes in. I can't do this.

You know, I'm secretly proud of you, he says.

He strides up the path, along our street, past all the windows.

There's big Colin away back to his work. Early the day, is he no?

I want to run behind him. Run in front of their windows in my second-hand silk kimono. *Who the hell does she think she is?* Spin him round, see his face when I scream at the pitch of my lungs.

Don't you dare be secretly proud of me. Don't you dare, you black-enamelled big bastard.

Scream for attention.

Are you listening, everybody? The big man has something to tell you. Come on, Colin, shout it out. *I am proud of my wife. I am proud of my wife.*

I don't. I close the door, and stand in the hall, alone. Not wanting to go back in to them. Unable to face their wee faces. Concentrate on what you have to do. Find out what's on telly for the wean. Check Carrie's verruca plaster. Try to be with Lisa before she takes off, again. Iron their school uniforms. Remember not to peel as many potatoes. Make it all right.

All day, I keep falling over them, they don't move from my side. Even Lisa stays in. She seems to have taken charge of the kettle.

Do you want coffee, Mum? Sit down, I'll make it.

Even at the dinner table, they're quiet, well-behaved children. I want them to behave normally; fight, kick under the table, stab each other with forks, flick peas. They are being good. I don't want them to be good. They shouldn't need to be good. I get up to clear away. David picks up his own plate, and follows me into the kitchen. I step back from the sink, and tread on him. Sorry.

He looks at me and says, Was it me?

What, son?

Was it cos I was up on the school roof? Is that how my daddy doesn't want to come back here? Is it cos I'm bad?

And your heart can break. It isn't just an expression, it can break. I feel mine snap in two, feel the pieces sink down to either side of my ribcage. Feel the emptiness where a heart used to be. I sit down on the floor and cradle my boy.

Oh no, no. It isn't you, you aren't bad, son. You're my beautiful boy. I love you. Your dad loves you. Honest, son. David, are you listening? I said honest.

He turns away. Oh, darling boy, don't.

Not knowing what else to say, I clamber up, take his hand and bring him with me, through the living-room, past his silent sisters, and out into the hall. I keep a tight hold on him as I lift the receiver and press the numbers. And when she answers, I say, over and over, Oh Bernie. Oh Bernie.

Now she is here.

She brought food and wine. She brought gardenia-scented soap. Water therapy. She runs the bathwater, puts out clean towels, searches in the bedroom for an outfit for the patient.

There you are: knickers, vest thing – I was looking for a bra, but then I remembered you don't wear them – big shirt, leggings. You get in there and relax, me and the weans'll do the dishes. I don't want to hear a cheep out of you for the next half-hour. Go on.

I lie in scented waters, observed by a parade of Lego men, lined up along the edge of the bath, on surveillance until David's bathtime. I can't relax. How the hell am I supposed to relax?

Close your eyes and think about nice things.

That's what my mother used to tell me when I couldn't sleep. Close your eyes and think about nice things.

Favourite film … *Bringing Up Baby*. Katherine Hepburn, hirpling along with a heel missing: *I was born on the side of a hill*. Cary Grant a gorgeous, bewildered academic.

Favourite words . . . Delight . . . Cataclysmic. Is that what this is, cataclysmic? Cataclysmic. Catatonic. Academic. Orgasmic.

No, not orgasmic. He was right; hardly the last of the red-hot lovers. They stopped. Even when I read all the right books, they refused to reappear. Or at least they refused to reappear when I wasn't alone. Bashful wee orgasms. We're not coming if he's here.

The wanting stopped as well. Not wanting him became a habit, like his drinking. Not wanting him because he was drunk, and not wanting him when he was sober, because he had been drunk. The resentment blocking all the desire, and the arousal, and the release. Other things got in the way too: kids, work, money, studying, boredom, especially boredom. But it was really that night, when I stood beside him in the lounge of the Crennan Arms, and I was talking to him, I wanted to tell him something, but he wasn't listening. He was feeling my arse and winking at the troops. That's what did it, that's what killed everything, just that.

I know.

He didn't rape me, he didn't kick my head in. I know that many a woman wouldn't think twice about a wee drunken grope from her own husband. I know. But surely I'm not the only woman in the whole of Saltcoats who doesn't find public humiliation arousing.

Nice things.

Music. CDs and cassettes all jumbled together. Eric Satie and Van Morrison, The Temptations and Patsy Cline, Buckwheat Zydeco and Beethoven.

Most embarrassing moment . . . buying CDs with my dad there.

Whit the hell's fire are ye lookin at Beith oven fur?

Nobody has ever escaped from Woolworths in

Dockhead Street as fast as I did that day. I have to tell my dad, but not today.

The water's cold. I sit up, use Bernie's soap. Soap and rinse, soap and rinse, step out. I wrap myself in the big towel, pulling it close around me, the way I used to with them.

Hurry hurry, rub-a-dub-dub, lift your arms up to the sky, dry in there, that's not tickly, it is not, wee fibber, hurry hurry, into your jammies. Sing a song, Mummy, sing a song.

Ma maw's a millionaire
Blue eyes and curly hair
Sitting among the Eskimos
Playing a game o dominoes
Ma maw's ... a ... millionaire.

I hear Bernie calling.

Is that you out, Lizzie? There's tea made when you're ready.

I'll be down in a minute.

I get dressed in the bedroom. In the mirror I can see a lassie, wearing blue knickers and a matching lacy vest, a lassie with a flat stomach and small breasts. Not a grown-up woman in sexy underwear, just a daft lassie that would never wear stuff like that.

EIGHT

I need some new notebooks. Clean, fresh paper. A new start. Sort everything out; make a plan. Pin it up on the wall. Separate ones for each paper. Write lists.

The student shop isn't too busy. A4 pads. Recycled? No, I hate the colour. Maybe I'd better. Pentels, fine point. Six. David 'borrows' them. Two large notebooks and a small one, for lists. Folders: red, green, yellow and blue. A notebook with a Monet cover. What for? Writing? *The Life and Times of Lizzie Burns?* The daft poetry hidden in the drawer?

The sweeties and crisps are all next to the till; same as Tesco.

Mummy, I want Smarties. Mummy, I'm taking these.

Mummy, I want want want.

Screaming, *Put it back. NOW.* Flushed and harassed.

Avoiding the eyes of the disapproving housewives.

Shouldnie huv them if ye canny control them.

Fuck off.

I'll take something home for them. No, not pastilles; she hates pastilles. Bonbons? Bad for their teeth … *Your ain wean suffers …*

Yorkies. I'll take three Yorkies for after their tea.

I go back to my table in the library.

I'm behind with my work. This term will be the one where I get myself together. I can't waste those other years. It'll be over soon. And I'll be able to sort out everything else. Now I need to work to a pattern. Catch up. Get it right.

Lynne appears at my side. She crouches down and says in a stage whisper, Come for a coffee, I need to talk to you.

I say, I can't. I'm busy. Can't it wait?

Elaine's here too.

Take a break, she says. You look knackered. Come on.

I allow myself to be led, collect books, bag and coat. I can't do this.

We go into the union, and Lynne goes up for the coffees. I don't belong here. I don't recognise the music that is pumping up through the floor and into my chest. Lynne sits down and launches into a tirade.

There's been another complaint about that bastard Sloan. A first year, of course. It seems that she went to see him because she'd failed her class exam. He offered her private tuition. And when she showed up for her 'tuition', he made his move.

I say, Who did she complain to?

Another tutor, Lynne says.

Elaine rakes her fingers through her hair, fired up for a fight.

Oh great. So it's just another rumour, and it'll get covered up like all the others.

It's been going on for years, I say. You'd need hidden cameras to nail that bastard.

Lynne shakes her head.

Lizzie, that's the attitude that allows him to get away with it. You can't just say that. Something has to be done.

Enough.

I say, Okay, Lynne, you do something. You get up off your arse and do something. And then, when you've done something, you can walk the half-dozen or so steps to your nice flat, and maybe Jack, or whoever the man of the moment is, will make you a nice dinner. And then you can study for as long as you like. And then you can both fall into bed and fuck all night. YOU do something, Lynne. I don't have time.

I grab my things and try to squeeze past, ignoring the looks on their faces. Christ, nobody uses the ashtrays in this place; the floor's a bloody mess. I head for the door.

Out on the steps, a youth attired like an extra from the cast of *Oliver* blocks my way. He thrusts a paper in my face.

Like to buy a copy of this week's *Socialist Worker*, dear?

Dear? I say. No. I would not. AND I'm not your dear. AND what the fuck would you know about work, you little wanker?

He teeters backward on the step, then rights himself and hurries off; desperate to escape this marauding madwoman. I hear Elaine behind me.

Lizzie. Lizzie, wait.

My eyes are watering, it must be the cold; I'm not buttoned up.

I say, Elaine, tell Lynne, tell her I'm sorry.

She knows, she says. We all know that you're under a lot of pressure.

No. I shouldn't have spoken to her like that. It's just that . . . any other time I would have advocated castration. Elaine, something's happened.

What? she says. What's happened?

And then there's the telling.

I say, It's Colin; he's left me. He says he can't put up with me any more. He says he's going to stay at his mother's when he comes back at the weekends. He says that the kids have to go there to see him. Oh, Elaine, how could he do that to his kids?

She puts her arms around me.

Oh, Lizzie. He hasn't just done it to his kids. What about you?

I'm fine. I'm just so worried about the kids. David thinks it's his fault; he actually asked me if it was his fault.

She says, Come back in. Come back in for a drink, and we'll talk.

I can't, I say. I have to go home.

Well, don't come in tomorrow, work at home. You can't cope with the travelling on top of everything else, you're shattered.

No, Elaine. If I stay at home I'll stay in bed, or I'll do the bloody housework or something. I have to keep coming up here. I have to keep doing this.

One day, she says. One day won't make any difference. Maybe you should just put the kids out to school and go back to your bed. Lizzie, you need a break.

No. Honestly, I'll be okay. Tell Lynne I'm sorry.

She says, I'll phone you tonight. Take care.

Yes okay. Thanks, Elaine. Bye.

I hurry down the hill and along the lane to the

Underground. The winos are there in the doorway of the bistro, huddled together in the warmth and the smells.

Hey, darlin. Cheer up. Giez a smile.

Up early. Get them out to school. Get myself onto a train. That's the hard part, getting on and staying on. Resist the urge to jump off at Kilwinning. No time for panic attacks. Wait for a space in my diary. Stay on the bloody train. Breathe deeply. Count backwards . . . ninety-five . . . ninety-four . . . Listen to the Walkman.

I am at peace.

Off the train at Central. Walk down Gordon Street, turn into Buchanan Street. Too early for the buskers. I saw the sign last week: *Standby Appointments*. One last extravagance.

A tiny girl, in combat trousers and a chiffon blouse, takes my coat and sits me down before a mirror.

Your stylist will be with you in just one minute. Would you like to see some style folios?

I avoid my own reflection by looking at pictures of impossibly beautiful women with impossible hairstyles. My stylist arrives. He is also impossibly beautiful, and very, very camp.

Hello there. My name's Carlo. We'll just have a chat first. I'll ask you a few questions, about your hair and your lifestyle. And you can tell me what you have in mind. And we'll take it from there. Okay? Lovely.

His own hair is russet-coloured. He wears leather trousers, draped with fine gold chains, and a tight white t-shirt. A gold Nefertiti hangs from one ear.

So, he says, let's take a look.

He lifts locks of hair. Probing, examining; reminding me of the nit nurse at school.

He says, What products have you been using?

Just shampoo and conditioner, I say. Whatever comes to hand.

I don't confess that sometimes I resort to Matey bubble bath, if the shampoo's run out.

Mmm, he says. Well, whatever it is, it's far too harsh. I'll recommend some of our range of products before you leave. Now, what did you have in mind?

I had running away in mind.

I say, I'm not too sure. I thought ... maybe ... something a bit more modern?

Exactly what I was thinking, he says. I saw you come in, and I thought, That woman would really suit something younger. Casual. You know? Where do you usually have it done?

The hick from the sticks replies, Just a wee place in Saltcoats. I live there.

He is encasing me in a black plastic wrap and purple towels.

Oh no, he says. I knew it. Is it a wee Senga's? I bet it is. You've got a definite touch of the Princess Di's there.

I can't help it. I'm laughing.

He says, I probably shouldn't have said that, should I? Honestly, I didn't mean to insult you. Now, I think we should go for something much softer. Wispy fringe. With it just coming on to your face at the sides, and at the nape. Much sexier. That okay? Lovely.

He calls out to chiffon blouse, Amber. Would you shampoo this client, please?

Amber shampoos. She shampoos rather well. No water cascades down my neck. No mascara runs down my cheeks. I am neither frozen nor scalded. The operation is quite painless.

That's you, she says.

She pats me kindly with more purple towels.

Carlo will be with you in a minute. Would you like tea or coffee?

Coffee please.

I sip my coffee. Carlo returns, Nefertiti swinging. He snips and teases and rubs. And he tells me about his Italian mother, and his holiday in Turkey. I light a cigarette and tell him about my finals. And I'm glad that is all he needs to know. I am a student, nothing more.

He says, I'll just let you finish your ciggy before I dry you. Or we'll both disappear in a flurry of fag ash.

And then he finger-dries me.

Just some mousse. About this much. Just scrunch it with your fingers; it should be no trouble. Wow. What do you think?

Someone else has appeared in the mirror: someone younger, lighter, with a wispy fringe and a smile.

It's great, I say.

It really suits you, Carlo says. The fringe shows up your eyes. Oh yes. Very sexy. You look about twenty-five. Oh, here, it would be a laugh if you were only twenty-four, wouldn't it?

I reassure him that I'm not twenty-four. And I confess that I can't afford any of their range of products.

Well, just you make sure that you come back here, he says. I don't want to find out that you've been back to wee Senga's. Take care. Bye now.

Hello, Lizzie. Did you have a good Christmas?

Oh yes, lovely.

Dr Brown sits opposite me, smiling and nodding. The break obviously did him good. I'll lay odds that he didn't get pissed and flatten the Christmas tree.

He says, I like your hair. You look like a girl, Lizzie.

Thank you.

Now, he says, this term is very important. You have quite a lot of work to do. And you've been taking far too long on your essays. From now on I want you to write them up in an hour.

I say, I can't write an essay in an hour.

Yes, you can. I don't mean the reading and taking notes, I mean writing up the material. The Brontë essay for instance, is it finished yet?

No. I can't seem to get it right.

It doesn't have to be right, Lizzie, but it does have to be written.

He's still smiling, but I think he means it.

He says, Don't look so stricken.

He looks at me for what seems like ages, then he begins shuffling papers.

He says, I know that it isn't easy for you, with your other responsibilities. I know that you're close to Rachel, have you tried talking to her about—er—things? Or, I could arrange for you to see the student counsellor, if you want to.

Poor man. He probably thinks that I'm about to weep all over him, or make a grab for his heart, mind and genitals, like that other married lady who caused him so much trouble.

I say, That won't be necessary; I'll see Rachel soon. I'll get down to the work. Next week I'll bring in the essay, and I'll try to work out some sort of agenda for the rest of the papers.

He looks relieved.

That's good. We'll work on a study plan for you. Don't worry, we'll get you through. I'm sure you'll do well.

I'm glad someone's sure of me.

I wander down to the Union, in search of company.

Elaine's there with some people from Sociology, including that prat Eddie. If he says bourgeois just once, I'll scream. I hug Elaine, then push through an assortment of Gothic children at the bar.

Back at the table, I interrupt a debate on sexuality.

Elaine's saying, Of course, we're all intrinsically bisexual.

Personally, I've never been able to get my good Catholic-lassie head round that one. I stay silent, listen to blasts of Nirvana, feeling like a parent who's wandered in by mistake.

The others drift off, until there's only Elaine and me and Eddie left.

I say, Elaine, do you fancy going somewhere else?

Aye, she says. We could walk down to the lane. We can't really talk in this place.

We're both hoping that Eddie won't tag along. He lifts his rucksack, with a great sense of purpose.

It's all right for some, he says, I've got to get to a tutorial. Hey, before I go, would you two like to come up to my place for something to eat some night? I can assure you, I'm hot stuff in the kitchen.

We plead babysitters and exams etc., but maybe after the finals. We'll definitely get back to him. Oh yes, definitely.

That's great, he says, I'll look forward to it. One more thing. You know what you were saying? Well, tell me, are lesbian orgasms more intense than heterosexual ones?

Elaine is slumped over the tabletop, shoulders shaking, giggles escaping through the fall of her hair. It's left to me to say it.

Eddie, we wouldn't know; we're not lesbians. And, even if we were, I doubt if we'd fancy a ménage à trois in *Govan* with *you*.

He backs away, stumbling and muttering.

It was what she said. I mean . . . I thought. And you two are very close, aren't you?

I say, Yes. Okay, Eddie, you're right. We are lesbians. If you are the alternative, then we're definitely lesbians. Now get lost.

We're still laughing when we get to the lane.

Oh Jesus, Elaine says, I've had many a proposition in this place, but that's the first time I've been asked to come wi my pal.

Elaine spoons the froth from her cappuccino.

Why don't we have a night out next week? You and Lynne could come up to my place for your tea, and then we could all go out for a drink. What do you say?

I'll need to see if Jill can stay on a bit later, I say. I can't really afford to pay her extra.

Elaine says, You shouldn't need to pay a babysitter. What about your dad? Or Colin's mother? Why don't you ask one of those two?

Because, I say, my dad never babysits. And I don't want that old bitch anywhere near my children. Anyway, do you think she'd look after them to let me go out hoorin it in Glasgow?

Ha ha, she says. That's a laugh. Maybe that's what you could be doing with.

What? Going out hoorin it?

No. I meant . . . you know, a wee bit of comfort. Should I invite Tony as well?

What's that supposed to mean?

Nothing, she says. But d'ye fancy him?

Don't be stupid, I say. I don't remember what that feels like. And somehow I can't see him playing Daddy to my three.

Lizzie, she says, you're priceless. I asked if you wanted to fuck the guy, no marry him. And your bairns don't need a daddy; they've got one. But maybe you could be doing with somebody.

I've just got rid of somebody, thank you very much. Now, can we change the subject? Talk about something intellectual. I need the stimulation.

Okay, she says. Did you see *Brookside* last night?

Sean comes in.

He says, I'm glad I caught you two. You're both invited to a party. Valerie and me are getting married on the fourteenth of April.

You're kidding, I say. That's two weeks before the finals start.

He says, I know. I'll sit my finals and then we're going to Rome. We just want to be married. Be together through it all.

Together.

He says, Here's Tony, he's going to be my best man.

Tony stands behind me.

Well, well, he says. What happened to you? You look like a wee lassie. It suits you. Fed up with the Doris Day look, were you?

Something like that. How's your dad? I say. Will you be able to get away for the wedding?

He says, He's actually a bit better. He's a fighter, always was. I'll make it to the wedding. And I'll leave the phone number so that they can reach me at Sean's place. My mother and our Donna said they would manage fine without me.

So, Elaine says, are we gonny have the pleasure of seeing you two in penguin suits?

No way, Sean says. We're just wearing jeans and shirts. Valerie's sister's making frocks for her and Valerie. But they're nothing elaborate. It'll just be the registrar's, then the piss-up at Val's parents' place later on.

I say. You mean, we're not having steak pie? And a band that plays 'Ten Guitars' and 'Jambalaya'?

Sean says, What the hell are you talking about?

She's talking about a real wedding, Elaine says. One wi two mothers in stupid-lookin hats. And an old uncle that feels the bridesmaids' arses. You mean you've never been to a wedding like that?

No, Sean says. I must have led a sheltered life. Thank Christ.

You don't know what you're missing, Elaine says. You should let us organise yours. I'm sure we could find you a nice shiny polyester suit, and some slip-on shoes and sports socks.

And we'll find you a guest that'll get totally pished, and shout, IRA ya bastards! Tony says. Or UDA, if you've invited a lot of Tims.

I say, And all the women'll throw Valerie up in the air, so that everybody can see her knickers. And then we'll all do the conga up the street. Then we'll have the last waltz. And then there'll be a fight. We'll have a great time.

Sean says, No thanks. Just you two turn up on the fourteenth. And no wedding presents. You can bring a bottle if you like.

Sorting the piles and piles of paper.

What's it all for? I'm the only one who cares. I want to

put it all into order: nine papers, nine folders. How many hours per paper? God knows.

Carrie limps in.

Mum, my foot's sore.

Oh, Carrie, what are we going to do with your feet?

She stands on one leg, accentuating her infirmity.

I say, I'm really busy just now, hen. Do you think you could wait a wee while? If I can just get all of this stuff sorted, then I'll see to your foot. Okay?

No, she says, my foot's really sore. You don't care, you only care about stupid university. I hate you. I hate everybody in this house.

She glowers at me. I used to be the only one who escaped the glowers. She was never what you would call a sunny child, but she smiled for me. When she was tiny, the only people she spoke to were Lisa and me; everyone else got the glowers, even her dad. The Infanta of the Perpetual Scowl. Even at playgroup, she played by herself in a corner. And when she started school she came home and said, *I don't like those children*. I was really the only one that she had any time for. Now she hates me too.

I say, You do not hate us. Stop being so twisted, Carrie. Sit down and I'll take your verruca plaster off.

No, she says. It'll be sore.

It's already sore, I say. The plaster's supposed to come off today. Let me take it off. And then we'll bathe your foot, and it'll be much better.

She sits on the floor with her foot on my lap, still glowering. I gently loosen the corner of the plaster, and she yelps.

Ow. Ow. Stop it.

Carrie, that was not sore. Now, this will only take a wee minute.

I pull it hard, and that is sore. Her lip is trembling, and silent tears begin to roll down her cheeks.

I don't like this. It hurts.

I hold out the plaster.

But look, I say, I've got it out.

She leans against me, and I feel her shoulders shaking.

No. Not that. THIS. I don't want to go to Nana's to see my dad. I hate this. I don't want to be different. I want to be the same as Ashley and Kerry. I want my mum and dad back.

I try to pull her up, but she remains rigid, pounding my thigh with her fist, sobbing into the folds of my skirt.

I hate this. Nobody asked me. Why did Dad not ask me?

I slip down beside her, hold her close.

Oh baby. Shush.

Weeping amongst the piles of paper. I never wanted them to see me cry. How can we miss him, when he hardly looked the road we were on? Rocking. Trying to stem her tears, while my own fall into the fire in her hair.

The plan is useless. The plan, the notepads, the wall chart; all useless. It doesn't matter. I'll fail, again. Read some, write some, keep going. Just keep going.

Last night I dreamed that I was pregnant. I was so relieved to be only pregnant. I can do that. No finals, just a baby. Oh, thank God. And today, I saw a couple of students, with their baby. The girl gave her child to his long-haired daddy, and went off to a lecture. I wanted to say, Give the baby to me, I know how to do that; I'm good at that.

I want my mum and dad back.

They wonder at my courage. *How does she do it?*

How do I do it?

I can't not do it. What else can I do? I can't go back;

there's nothing else. I have to see it through to the end, sit my finals. Then what? Little children who need their mother. How can I dismiss them as nothing?

I will pay for this. One day they will accuse me. Accuse me of selfishness, of driving their father away, of ruining their childhoods, their lives. And I will plead guilty. Guilty and penitent, awaiting sentence.

The punishment will fit the crime. I will be condemned to solitary freedom. Alone. Unfettered. Middle-aged. Childless. A monster roaming free.

A life sentence.

NINE

Every seat in the library is taken. All around me are people with hunched shoulders and pinched faces. What are they thinking? Those two over there: she has blue hair and rag-doll clothes; he is a skinny boy with wire-rimmed spectacles. They've been walking around, hand in hand, for weeks.

They look like the children in that programme that David used to watch. What were they called? Rosie and Jim.

Oh Rosie, we're lost. What's going to happen to us?

'*Don't worry, Jim. We'll find a way. We'll be home in time for tea.*'

I wonder what careers they have planned? Will her blue hair make a difference? What are you going to be, Rosie?

A letter came this morning, Sarah's dead.

Her husband wrote: *Sarah took her own life on the 20 of October*.

I only met him once, he seemed nice enough. I didn't really know Sarah that well. We met last year, she was finishing the degree she had started years earlier. We talked, swapped life stories; congratulating each other on being survivors.

Poor Sarah, marriage and university both second attempts. I wonder if her suicide was a second attempt?

She told me about her first marriage and the baby, about the periods of mental illness, the spells in hospital, the hallucinations. She even showed me the wild, beautiful poetry, written when she was someone else.

My name is Sky.

But she didn't tell me that she wanted to die.

She was better. Recently remarried, and back to finish her degree with only the pretty pillbox containing a minimum dosage to show where she had been.

She was in love. She said she no longer wanted or needed the angry, feminist texts with which I armed myself.

But she believed in me. I remember her sitting on the wall outside the library, wrapped up in her big tweed coat and the red scarf that she had brought back from Moscow, laughing at my opinions on the men who inhabit academia.

Oh Lizzie, you're brilliant. I'll see your name in print one day.

Not now.

Why, Sarah? Why? If you were content in a cottage with your love? Did Sky come back? Sky wrote mad, wild, wonderful poetry. Your husband wrote,

Sarah graduated MA Arts after two resits.

And he signed that terrible letter, the letter telling me that you are dead,

Cheers for now, Ian.

Sky wouldn't have been able to live with a man like that. She was too far above him.

Oh God, no. The fire alarm. That bloody noise that makes you want to kill people just to get them out of your way, just to get away from it. No one moves. It persists. They make tentative gestures, shuffling papers, then standing up. Pretending that they were leaving anyway. A security guard strides up and down.

Right, ladies and gentlemen. Move towards the stairs, please. Make no attempt to use the lifts. Move forward, now. Use the stairs, please.

Seven flights. We move forward in orderly lines. Abandoning our valuables: study notes and texts, highlighted in yellow and green. I don't see anyone that I know.

Six.

Five.

Four.

It's okay. Soon. Just breathe. Relax. Don't panic. Count backwards from ninety-nine. Why? I read it in a book. Ninety-eight. Ninety-seven. I can see Rosie's blue hair. *Hello, Rosie, may I borrow Jim for a minute? I need to hold his hand.*

Two.

One.

Out.

I can hear my own breathing, my own heartbeat. And the voices, so many voices, everyone talking at once.

My bag's still in there.

It's only a drill.

This is all I bloody need.

Buy me a coffee.

Might as well go to the pub.

I sit down on the steps, just as Tony comes out, empty-handed.

I say, Did you leave all your stuff in there?

No, he says, I didn't have any stuff, I just nipped in for a book. I'm just up; I was working late last night.

I'm looking for Elaine, I say. Have you seen her?

He says, She's away up to see her tutor. I just met her on the hill.

But she hates her tutor, I say, sounding like Carrie.

Yeah, he says, smiling, but she still needs him. Anyway, how are you?

I'm fine.

Aye, Elaine said that you would say that. How can you be fine, Lizzie? Your man's just walked out on you. You're anything but fine.

What else do you want me to say, Tony? My man was about as much use as a chocolate teapot. And I have to concentrate on my kids and my finals. I don't have time for a nervous breakdown. But okay, you win. Right now I can't breathe, and I can't move, and my stuff's still in the library, and I feel absolutely awful, and I need to find Elaine.

He says, What do you need to see her for?

Do you remember Sarah? I say.

Aye, he says. Long red hair. Has she left? I haven't seen her about.

I got a letter from her husband this morning. She's dead.

He sits down next to me, takes hold of my hand.

Fuck, Lizzie. How?

I say, I just know that she killed herself; he didn't say how. The tears that have been threatening since breakfast time fill my eyes. I turn away from him. He stands up, tugging at my hand.

C'mon, he says. We're going for a walk. You can't do this here . . .

Tony, I say, you don't need to look after me. I'll be fine.

Christ, he says. Look, I know I don't fucking need to look after you, I need to get away from here, and so do you. Now move.

We go to the park. We walk round the duck pond, past all the statues of famous men. Halfway round we sit down on a bench. Across the way a large flock of pigeons perch on the branches of a tree. An officious-looking assembly, a parliament of pigeons.

I say, Tony, I don't want to cry. I'm just so bloody angry . . .

Aye, he says, that's understandable.

You know, I say, she actually thought that married bliss would make it all better. She stopped writing poetry, she stopped reading all the books that might have helped her. She didn't even get the degree she deserved. She shut herself away in a bloody cottage with her loving husband, and she gave up. No fucking wonder she killed herself. She had no life. Did she?

He says, What the hell are you talking about, Lizzie?

Sarah, I'm talking about Sarah. She gave up, opted for a conventional wee life. That's why she killed herself; she couldn't bear it.

He stands up, the pigeons fly off.

Turning, he says, Christ, I don't believe you. Sarah was

ill, mentally ill. She'd been hospitalised umpteen times. You can't blame her fucking husband. The guy loved her; if it hadn't been for him she'd probably have topped herself long before now.

How can you know that, Tony? You have no idea.

He turns and walks away, black coat billowing out behind him. I rise to follow him but he turns, shouting.

I was there the day she went mad in the coffee bar. He was late arriving to pick her up. She took a dive at the poor guy, clawing at his face with her nails, punching and kicking, screaming all kinds of abuse. The place was packed out, everybody looking at them. And do you know what he did? Eh? He talked to her. He tried to keep her at arm's length, and he talked to her. Softly, just, *It's okay, my love, it's okay*, over and over, till she got a bit quieter, till she stopped kicking and screaming. Then, when she would let him, he held her tight, stroked her hair, and got her out of there. Blood pouring from his face, all those staring bastards enjoying the show. I asked him if he needed a hand getting to the car, and he asked if I would pick up Sarah's things, her bag and her books and stuff. When he was strapping her into her seatbelt, she reached up and touched his scratches. Sorry, she said. And again all he said was, *It's okay, my love*. I remember I said something feeble like, Will you be all right?, and he said, Yes. That's all, just yes. I've never felt so sorry for anyone in my life So don't try and turn Sarah into some kind of feminist martyr. She was ill for years and she killed herself. Her husband loved her and he tried to help her, but he couldn't. It's all very sad, but really it's got nothing to do with you. I'm sorry, Lizzie, but you can't take that woman's life and death and turn her into fucking Sylvia Plath. Now can we go back? I'm choking for a coffee.

I follow him, scattering pigeons from my path. I'm still angry, but not at him, or Sarah's husband. I'm just angry and sad and ... God knows. I expect Tony to leave me at the coffee bar but he goes up to the counter and asks for two coffees, so I find us a table. He sits opposite me, silently staring into his coffee cup. He's angry too. To fill the silence I ask about his dad.

He says, He doesn't want to go back into hospital, and my mother wants him at home. I've been trying to help out. I go back home as often as I can. In fact, I'm going to pack in the job in the Union. I'll need to keep the flat on, but I'll spend as much time as I can with them.

Do you think that you'll be able to sit your finals? I say. God, Tony, I'm sorry, that's probably the least of your worries.

No, he says, I've made up my mind, I'm definitely going to sit them.

Are you sure you'll be able to?

'I'll probably fuck it up, he says, but I'm going to sit them. You see, it was the other night, I was back home, and I'd been sitting with my dad, just talking to him. I went to make a cup of tea, and my mother came into the kitchen. She said, He really wants you to get your degree, Anthony. He's really proud of you, son. She went away, and I stood there at the sink, thinking, I can't, I can't handle it. But later on I went into their bedroom. He was in bed, and she was lying on top of the covers with her arms round him. They were sleeping. And the way she was lying, her skirt had moved up round her thighs. And I thought, God, she's got beautiful legs. She looked like a young lassie, then I thought, She was. She was a lassie with beautiful legs and a great smile. And he was a young guy, working on the railways, and following Celtic on a Saturday. And they fell in love and got married and had kids, and they were bloody good to us. Our Donna turned out fine, but I gave them nothing but grief. Smoking dope and dropping acid, and pissing off to London for two years, and then Europe for another four. Half the time they didn't know whether I was alive or dead. And I thought to myself, Right, McGuire, you're going to sit your finals. For their sake, you owe them that much.

I say, Have you told your tutor about your dad?

No, he says. What's it got to do with him?

Well, it could affect your results, Tony. In fact, it probably will. If you tell your tutor what's happening, it'll go on record that you sat your exams under bloody awful circumstances. Then, if you do mess up, they'll look at your work. They'll look at your essays before they make a decision about your degree. You should go and see him.

Aye, he says. Maybe I will. The thing is, though, I don't know how long my dad's going to hang on for. He could be dead and buried by the time I sit them.

I know, I say. Then it would have to go on record that you had recently been bereaved. Tony, you have to tell them. Are you listening to me?

Okay, I will. Should you not do the same, though?

What?

He says, You'll need to tell your tutor about what's happening at home. I mean, I don't want to be nosy, but is Colin coming back?

I don't know, Tony. I don't know.

Elaine arrives.

Where've you two been? she says. I've been looking everywhere for you. Were you in the library when the alarm went off, Lizzie?

Aye. I nearly had a breakdown walking down all those stairs. I met Tony outside, and we went for a walk.

Tony says, Are they letting people back in yet, Elaine?

Aye, she says, it was only a drill.

Right then, he says, I'm going to get that book, and head back home.

He stands up and puts his coat on.

I don't know when I'll be back in, he says. Listen, if you see Sean, tell him I'll give him a bell when I get the chance. Okay? Bye, Elaine. Lizzie, you take it easy. I'll see you later. Bye.

Elaine brings out her packed lunch. She's vegetarian; really into all the healthy stuff. Healthy-eating and exercise, aerobics and swimming and meditation. She's always on at me to do something; go to one of her classes with her. I don't have time. She bought me some herbal teas, and some Rescue Remedy.

She says, You two must have had a bloody long walk; I was looking for you for ages.

I don't want to tell her about Sarah. I don't want to talk about it now.

Aye, we did. I tried to find you when I came out of the library, but Tony said that you'd gone up to see your tutor. How was he?

Oh, nearly human, she says. I'd got myself into a state about one of my papers. He was really good; sat down and talked it through with me. I feel a lot better now. Anyway, what about you? How are you?

I'm fine, I say. I just got a bit panicky when the fire alarm went off.

She's polishing a big red apple on the sleeve of her top. I can't remember the last time I did that, primary school probably.

She says, I wish you would stop saying that. You can't be fine. How can you be fine, Lizzie? Have you spoken to Colin? D'ye know what's happening? I mean, is that it? He's never coming back?

I say, Christ knows. I'm so worried about the kids. Poor wee Carrie was breaking her heart the other night, and David thinks that it's his fault. Lisa's walking around as if nothing's happened. But she must be feeling it, I know she must.

She says, Don't you think that you should defer your exams? You could sit them next year, when you've got everything sorted.

NO.

I startle myself, as well as Elaine and half the folk in the coffee bar.

I say, I can't, I can't give up. If I give up, it'll all have been for nothing. If I give up, I'll have to go back there and face everybody. I can't.

Okay, she says, it was only a suggestion. But you'll have to get some help. You can't do it all on your own.

I say, I'm sorry, Elaine. I know you're only trying to help. But honestly, I'll be all right. I've got Jill and Bernie. Everything'll work out. I mean, look at poor Tony. His dad's dying.

I know, she says, it's a shame. When you think about it, it's just no bloody fair. All the hassle you go through, coming here as a mature student. And life just goes on, with all the responsibilities, and all the problems. I don't have kids, though. I don't know how the hell you've managed. That reminds me. Guess what?

What?

She says, You know that Nick has asked me to go to the States with him.

Aye. Are you going?

She smiles, Uh huh.

I say, For how long?

Don't know, she says, we'll take it as it comes. And, when I get back I want to have a baby.

Christ, I say. Nick's baby?

If he's still around. I just know that I want my own baby.

She puts her feet up on the chair, pulls her knees up to her chest and wraps her arms around them.

And I also know that I'm sick of being good: my mother's good wee lassie, good wee nurse, Martin's good wee girlfriend. I'm going to go for what I want. I'm going to be like you, Lizzie.

I can't believe she's saying this.

I say, Are you crazy? Like me? I've fucked everything up. My kids will grow up to be emotional cripples. I've got one with a psychosomatic limp; one running along roofs on suicide missions; and one hurtling through puberty with every reason to hate the sight of me. And now, I've driven their father away. Do whatever you want to do Elaine, but for Christ's sake, don't model yourself on me.

She's up on her feet now. Her hair has escaped from the pins that usually keep it piled up; and now it's falling, tumbling down over her shoulders.

She says, Oh Lizzie, shut up. You didn't drive their father away. God, there's plenty of guys that would give their fucking eye-teeth to have a woman like you. And as for the kids; they'll grow up knowing that their mother was true to herself, and loved them to bits in the process. Listen, I've had the career, I've done the degree, nearly. And next I'm going to have a break, and hopefully, a baby. Your next step is a career.

Oh aye, I say. Careering right off the top of that tower

up there, or careering right off Saltcoats harbour. Take your pick.

Good one, Lizzie. Just perfect in the circumstances.

I dodge the slap she aims at my head.

Okay, I'm sorry, don't hit me. You go for it. I'll be there for you when the time comes.

I know, she says. She starts shoving her hair back up; anchoring it with the pins.

Oh, I nearly forgot. I met Sean. He says to tell you that there's a note on the board in your department; you've to go and see Dr Brown as soon as possible.

Shit. I'm avoiding him. I want to go over there all in control and organised. Bugger that bloody fire alarm.

My dad paces the floor. He's not happy.

In the name o God. There's nae need for this. Nae need at all. Whit the hell are ye gonny dae? An they poor weans. Whit aboot them?

I say, I'll do what I've always done, Dad. I'll cope, I'll manage. And the weans will be fine. Colin was never bloody there. But of course, you never noticed that, did you?

He burls round, his face dark and twisted. He gets out of control when he can't control me.

Whit I noticed wis you and yer high-falutin ideas. Mibbe that's why he wis never there. Because you wurnie a wife tae him. He's no a bad man.

Oh, but I'm a bad woman; is that it? Look, Dad, I've told you now, okay? I thought you should hear it from me, before you heard it from some venomous bastard in the pub. Now I'm off.

I reach for my coat. Auntie Jean, here on her usual Saturday visit, intervenes.

Aw, hen, sit doon. I'll make us a wee cup of tea. C'mon now, Tam. The lassie's upset enough. It's a wee bit of support she's needing, no you rantin and ravin like a bloody heid case.

He stands between us, shaking his head. And then I see the tears. He puts his arms round me, and he's crying.

Aye, greet away, Tam.

Oh, hen, I'm that sorry. But mibbe it's no too late. Could ye no try again?

No, Dad. I can't try any more.

He gets up, in search of a hankie or something. I hear him talking to Auntie Jean in the kitchen.

Elisabeth drinks coffee, Jean. I keep a wee jar for her in that press up there.

I've ruined his Saturday. He hasn't even picked out his horses; his paper is lying, still folded, on the table. Auntie Jean brings the cups through. We sit sipping in silence.

She says, Where are the weans the day?

I've just dropped them off at Colin's mother's. He's staying there this weekend.

Well, that'll give you some time tae yourself, hen.

Aye.

My dad says, If ye've no got the weans, you could come round tae the club wi us.

No, I'm sorry, Dad, I can't. I have to get back up the road. I've got a lot of studying to do.

Studying? he says. Whit dae ye mean, studying? You mean yer no gonny leave the college, noo this has happened?

Christ Almighty, I can't handle this. There is absolutely no point in me even trying.

No, I say, my exams are in six weeks. I won't be leaving the University until they're over, Dad.

I don't know, he says. I don't know whit'll happen tae ye. I jist don't know.

I'll be fine, Dad. Don't worry about me.

I get ready to leave. More hugs and tears. I cross the road; turning to wave back at the window, where he stands watching, the way he used to when I crossed the road to school.

I lied about the studying. I'm meeting Bernie. We'll have lunch, and then look round the Saturday market. I couldn't have gone to the club with my dad and Auntie Jean if you'd paid me. I don't fit in there any more. I wish I did.

I wish that I could go back; turn back the clock and make it all right again. Go back to being the same as everyone else. Take away the pain and the guilt. Give my children their family back.

I want my mum and dad back.

Shush.

Back to when it was all safe and secure. And nothing ever happened. And I was glad of it. I want to be her again. I want to fit in. Where do I fit in? Nowhere.

I can't send my children out to play in a street where they are the only ones with no daddy. They don't want to be different, special. Neither do I.

What the hell did I think I was doing when I started this? Did I think that I could be like Rachel, with her big house and musician husband? Or like Lynne and Elaine, with their futons and Indian throws? I don't fit in up there either. I don't have a cheese plant, or a cafetiere, or a poster of Che Guevara in the hall. I don't have a radio permanently tuned to Radio Four. I don't have dinner at seven. I make the bloody tea at five.

Jesus, Lizzie, what have you done? But I can't go back. I can't unlearn it all. I can't pretend that I haven't read those books; had those conversations. I can't not know about Plato and Socrates, Joyce and Yeats, Kristeva and Cixous. I can't. Just like I can't stop preferring fusilli alla matriciana to tatties and mince, or the *Guardian* to the *Daily Record*, or Chianti to a nice wee bottle of Lambrusco, hen.

I thought I was so clever. A real character, defiantly tasting the strange bright fruits of knowledge. Now I swallow bitter aloes.

Bernie's waiting at the bus stop. She only gets one Saturday a month off. I bet she would rather have spent it with Frank, instead of her neurotic pal.

She says, Hi, doll. How'd it go with your dad?

Don't ask.

We walk round to the wine bar. That's a laugh. It only stocks two kinds of wine, and they're pish, but the name above the door impresses the tourists. My dad used to frequent this place when it was still just another bar on the corner. Now it has photocopied copperplate menus and the occasional candle stuck in a bottle. He would hate it. I doubt if the food would be to his taste either. *Three quid fur the skin aff a tattie?*

When we're settled with a couple of lasagnes, Bernie asks, So, what did auld Tam have to say?

The usual, I say. I'm a terrible wumman, and it's all my fault. Auntie Jean was there. She gave him a real bawling out, and he calmed down a bit. Then we had the tears; he's that worried about me. He doesn't have a clue, Bernie. He expects me to leave university, 'Noo this has happened'.

Don't let him get to you, she says. He's a different generation. He'll accept it eventually.

Aye. But will I?

Why? she says. What's up?

I just feel so guilty, Bernie. Constantly guilty. I feel guilty when I go to university; I feel guilty when I stay at home; when I shout at the kids; when I lose patience with my dad. I even feel guilty about Colin. I've taken his home and his family away from him. Why couldn't I have been content with what I had? I've been so bloody selfish. What have I done to them?

She leans across the table, takes hold of my arm.

Stop it, she says. Stop it right now. You've done nothing to them. Do you hear me? Selfish, my arse. You listen to me. I've kent you since you were just a wee lassie. Your mother had just died, and you were a poor wee thing. I've watched you for the past thirteen years: and all you've done is take care of other folk.

No, I say. I did what I wanted. I wanted kids, and I had them; I wanted to go to night classes, and I went; I went to university. I thought I was so clever. I didn't think about anybody else.

She says, And what about all the years before that? You raised those weans yourself, and waited hand and foot on big Colin at the same time. You ran up and down that hill to your father's when you were pregnant, and when you had one in the pram and one hanging on to either side of it. And where were they? Eh? Where were your dad and Colin, when you were running yourself ragged? I'll tell you where they were. They were holding up the bar in the Crennan. And that's what's bloody wrong with the pair of them. When you did something for yourself, they lost their wee skivvy. I don't want to hear any more of this 'selfish' crap. You've got to study for your exams. Me and Frank'll help you with the weans. I've already put in for a week's holiday, at the end of next month. So, get a grip. And get on with what you have to do. Okay?

I say, Aye, I suppose so.

There's no suppose about it, she says. Now I'm going for a pee. Order some hot chocolate fudge cake with fresh cream. As if my arse wisnie big enough, eh? You have some as well. You're okay; there's no a pick on you. And another two glasses of that cheeky wee whatever it is. I'll be back in a minute.

More wine, dessert, coffee. I wonder how the kids are getting on with Colin? Maybe he'll have taken them out somewhere. I hope to God we don't bump into them.

I say, How are Linda and Garry these days?

They're fine, Bernie says. We haven't heard from Garry in a while. You'd think he was at the other end of the earth, instead of just down the road in Irvine. He does work long hours, though. And he's going out with a nice wee lassie. Frank's always telling me, you can't hang on to them. Linda's supposed to be coming down tomorrow. Her and her washing.

When do her exams start? I say.

Not until the beginning of June, she says. I hope she manages to get a job. I don't know what the situation is with hotel management, whether there's plenty of jobs going or not. She'll be some manager. She always was a right wee bossy knickers. Remember?

Aye, she was very independent, wasn't she? Really different from Garry.

She says, I remember him screaming blue murder on his first day at school. The year before, she'd skipped in, no problem. Bye, Mum, and that was it. He was brokenhearted every day for a fortnight. I thought I was going to have to take him to a child psychologist. Now I'm lucky if I see him once a month. It just shows you, hen. You can't live your life for them, because they grow up and leave you on your arse.

We fight over the bill, and she wins.

She says, You can take me to the Savoy when you're earning a fortune.

We take a stroll round the market. I haven't been down here for months. It's more bother than it's worth if I have to bring David. He pesters me for toys that get broken before we get them home. Bernie buys a couple of house-plants, and I pick up some underwear for the lassies.

We pass by the man demonstrating miracle carpet-cleaner. The guy who sells the sheets and towels is giving his usual spiel.

Right. All youse snobs wi the avocado bathroom suites. There a lovely set of green towels. One bath sheet, two bath size, two hand. All for a tenner. I'm aff ma heid. Crazy prices. Just hand yer cash tae wee Tracy here.

At quarter to five, I say, Bernie, I'll need to run. I'm supposed to be collecting the weans at five. Listen, thanks for lunch and everything. You've really cheered me up. I'll pay you back one day.

She says, You don't have to pay me back. Just you look after yourself, and I'll see you during the week. Cheerio, hen.

I reach Colin's mother's house at one minute past five. Carrie and David are at the window, watching. They appear at the door with their coats on. May stands behind them.

I say, Where's Lisa?

David says, My nana was in the kitchen and Lisa went to the toilet and then she came back and said, Tell Nana I'm away to Kirsten's, and she just went away and I think she was cryin.

Where was your dad?

Carrie says, He was away out.

I look at May.

Where is he?

She says, He went for a couple of pints. The boy has to see his friends. You've taken everything else away from him. Lisa was just in one of her moods. She'll be in her pal's house. She's needing her backside skelped, if you ask me.

How could he? The bastard. And as for this old witch . . .

I say, I'm not asking you. And if you ever lay a finger on any of my children, you will be a very sorry old woman.

I grab the kids.

C'mon, you two. We're going to find Lisa.

I turn back at the gate. And I tell Mrs Burns, When your drunken bastard of a son comes home, you tell him to phone me.

I take my two sad-faced wee souls home. All the time fighting down the rage that threatens to rise up and blow us all away. I don't know what I'll do if she isn't at Kirsten's. If she isn't at Kirsten's, if she's run away, if she's gone missing, I'll kill him.

The phone rings just as I'm opening the door. It's Bernie.

Hello, Lizzie? I've just got in. Lisa's here. Frank says that she arrived about half-past three. She thought that you would be here.

Oh thank God. Is she okay?

She's fine. Frank thought she seemed a bit upset when she got here, but he gave her something to eat and he's had her helping him paint the garage. Did something happen with her and her dad?

Her dad fucked off to the pub, and left them with his mother. David says that Lisa just took off. I've been worried sick.

That man hasn't got the brains he was born with. What the hell's the matter with him? Listen, hen. I'm going to seven o'clock Mass, but Frank'll bring the wean home. You try and stay calm. I'll phone you later on. Bye.

I tell the other two.

Your sister's fine. She's round at Auntie Bernie's. She's been helping Uncle Frank to paint the garage.

I wish I'd been with Uncle Frank, Carrie says. It would have been better than sitting with my nana.

David starts jumping up and down.

Can I help Uncle Frank? Can I? Can I go round now? Can I, Mum?

No. It's too late now. Your Uncle Frank's bringing Lisa home in a wee while. When he gets here you can ask if you can help him another day.

A wee while later, Frank ushers Lisa in.

There you go. One daughter, safe and sound. Don't worry, hen, she didn't get her claes dirty; I gave her a pair of my overalls.

Lisa says, It was good fun. We got it finished, Mum.

That's great, hen.

We exchange a look that says, Later.

It's eight o'clock when Colin phones.

What's happening? he says.

What's fucking happening? Your daughter's all right, if that's what you mean. If you are enquiring about your own child, then yes, she is fine. No thanks to you. How dare you bugger off to the pub and leave them?

What? Do you expect me to stay in all day on a Saturday, just because they're coming down?

Yes. Yes, I do. I expect you to behave like a father. I expect you to be there for those kids.

No. Tell the truth. You expect me to baby-sit, so that you can go out on the piss wi your pal. Have a good time in Maxwell's, did you?

So, the troops were out in force with their walkie-talkies, were they? You are unbelievable, Colin. Absolutely fucking unbelievable. Don't call here again. **EVER**.

I slam the phone down. You've done it again, Lizzie. Scarlet woman. Talk of the town.

Lisa's standing in the doorway.

I say, I thought you were upstairs. Did you hear?

Yes, she says. Just ignore him.

Somebody told him that I was in the wine bar with Auntie Bernie. We were having lunch, Lisa. We had a couple of glasses of wine, but we were in there having lunch.

It doesn't matter, she says. You can go where you want. I'm never going to speak to him again.

I say, Why did you leave your nana's today?

She sits down opposite me. Don't bite your nails, hen.

She says, I didn't know if I should tell you this. That's why I went to Auntie Bernie's, I was going to ask her. Then I was doing the painting with Uncle Frank, and I thought, Why can my dad not be like him? I mean, Uncle Frank gets drunk. And sometimes he's funny, and other times he fights with Auntie Bernie, but he's really nice. And I stopped feeling worried. I just felt happy.

She chews on a thumbnail. Don't.

I say, You *should* feel happy, Lisa. But if you keep whatever it is that is upsetting you locked up inside, then you won't be happy.

She says, Okay. My dad went to the pub, Mum. He was supposed to be with us, and he went to the pub. He left us watching old black-and-white films with Nana. David was fed up, and my nana kept checking him for not sitting at peace. And Carrie just stopped speaking to her, you know what she's like. I didn't want to be there, I didn't want those two to have to be there. It's not fair, Mum. I know it's not your fault, but I'm not going to do that every Saturday, and I don't think you should make Carrie and David go either. My dad doesn't care about us. Don't send us down there again.

I don't know what to say to her.

She says, I hate him.

I say, You don't hate him, you're just feeling very hurt.

I put my arms around my big girl, and we hold on tight.

I say, Don't worry, Lisa. I won't make you go again.

TEN

I'm suddenly awake.

Lying perfectly still, perfectly straight.

Legs together, arms stretched out wide. And the tears which are stopped in daylight flowing down my cheeks and on to my neck. Trickling over the angry rash that rests above my collarbone.

Tears from the dream.

I have arranged a party; a very tasteful party. Good food and wines, beautiful flowers and tinkling music. But people huddle in groups and criticise.

The guest of honour arrives. My mother. She wears a simple black dress, and her hair is pulled back in a chignon. Death has granted her the elegance she coveted in life.

I say, Look. I did all of this for you. Are you happy with me? Are you pleased?

But she looks at me with such contempt, such scorn and disapproval, that I sink to my knees and sob. And now I'm awake, lying here, crucified on the marital bed.

I go downstairs. We've run out of tea bags and milk. I drink black coffee. I'll have to go to the shops later, or leave money and a list.

I open the blinds and sit in the chair. Nursing a mug, and looking out at the moon. A perfect full moon.

The rent's due. The phone bill came today. No, yesterday. I told him that I didn't want his money. Just give me enough for the kids, I said. Bernie thinks I'm a fool. I'll collect my last grant next month. What the hell will I do until then?

I watch the yellow moon change to pale then blushing pink, before it sinks and disappears behind the fields.

On the train, I plan the day ahead. First, the library, to find books for the Twentieth-Century Lit paper. I spent too much time on Joyce last year. Loving the books. You're not supposed to love them. You're supposed to read, dissect, and quote the authorities. Then a tutorial with Dr Brown, Jim. I can never think of him as Jim. I'm sure that he despairs of me. Why not? I despair of myself.

After that, I'll go and see the doctor at the student medical centre. I need a magic pill. Something to blot out the dreams and the tears, soothe the rash and loosen the knots. Something to lessen the tension.

The youth sitting opposite accidentally kicks my leg. I wince at the impact of his DM on my shin.

Ow! Fuck.

He blushes and stammers.

Sorry. Really sorry.

Poor thing. Too tall for his wee-boy face; as if someone

had taken a primary-school wean and stretched it.

I say, It's okay. Don't worry about it.

I'm getting old. Rushes of maternal feelings for clumsy youths? David will look like that one day. He'll stretch and grow, taller and taller, until he's a big man. By then they'll hate me. They'll leave, and I'll be left alone.

I feel the terror starting. *Sit it out, just sit it out. You know what to do. Breathe. Only one more stop. Count backwards.*

Ninety-nine.

Ninety-eight.

The train jars, jolts. We've hit something. Oh, Mother of God. The kids. I'm flung out of my seat. Sharp pain as my face slams against the boy's bony knee. The train screeches and stops. Strangers entangled: dignities askew, possessions adrift.

The driver, his mate, and the ticket collector work their way through the carriages.

It's okay now, folks. Nae need tae panic. Just a wee bump. Some idiot put a car seat on the line. Is anybody hurted?

I'm hurted, but I say nothing. There don't appear to be any real injuries, and after the train has been checked for damage, we move off again.

The big boy says, Are you okay? You banged your face on my knee; I'm sorry.

I say, It's all right, I'm fine now. What about you?

Bit shaky, he says. You get on these things every day, and you forget that this can happen.

Yes, I say, it's easy to forget.

The train pulls into Central. The big boy smiles and shoulders his rucksack.

That's us then. Cheerio.

I walk down the platform. Stepping out in jig time to

the bloody stupid Scottish music that they play at this time of the morning.

> *Rum tee tum tee tee tee tee tum tum tum,*
> *We're no awa tae bide awa.*

I wonder if they time it for the London train leaving?

I stop outside the coffee shop. I could go in but my hands are too shaky to hold a cup.

Breathe. Just breathe.

A woman comes out, elbowing past, her hands full with carrier bags, famous names facing outwards. She's wearing clothes similar to mine; jacket, shirt, trousers. But better, more expensive. I move out of her way. She turns, Thank you, and smiles. It's her. Me with designer labels and a mask of foundation, mascara and lipstick. Same haircut, only smoother, shinier, perfectly groomed. I look at her hand, her left hand, gripping the slim rope handle of a Hennes bag, diamonds and gold on her third finger. A married woman, a wife. Now she's walking away, same stride as mine, only her heels are higher.

My heart is banging away beneath my ribcage. I close my eyes and when I open them she's gone. Where? Is she who I'm supposed to be? A wee bit care and attention and you too could look like a million dollars, my lady. No. I need to get out of here, I have to find – someone – anyone. I can't face the buses or the Underground. To hell with the money; I'll have to get a taxi.

I get a nice cheery driver. I was hoping for one of the morose ones that take you there and take your money and that's it.

Glasgow Uni, eh? Whit dae ye dae up there, doll?

I tell him, and he starts going on about his wife doing social work at college.

She loves it, so she does.

The wee bump must have dislodged something, because my nocturnal tears are flowing in broad daylight, in a fast black going up Hope Street.

The driver says, Aw, hen, c'mon, it canny be that bad. Exams is it?

I say, Aye, it's exams.

We stop on University Avenue, and the driver says, Don't let it get to you, darlin. You get yourself a wee cuppa tea.

Undone by the kindness of strangers, I stand outside the gates, not knowing where to go. Rachel. Rachel knows.

There's a note pinned to her door.

All students

I will not be available until 17 April. Please direct all enquiries to Dr J. Brown, room 22–3.

Rachel Wilton

The door of room 22–3 is open. Jim is inside, standing by the window. He turns and sees me.

Lizzie? I thought our tutorial was at two.

I say, I have to see Rachel. Where is she?

The tears. I can't stop them. He comes out into the corridor.

What's the matter, Lizzie? What's happened?

I say, Where's Rachel? I need to see Rachel.

He says, Rachel had to take some leave. Her mother is ill. Come in here for a minute, sit down. What the hell's happened to you?

Another kind man. I try to say something intelligent, articulate, coherent, but instead I sob. I lay my head down and I sob all over James Brown's desk.

Lizzie, he says, tell me.

Tell you? I don't know what to tell you. There was an accident, the train, but it was nothing. This is – there's a woman – I don't know. I don't know what's happening to me. I'm sorry, Jim, I shouldn't be here. I should go home.

I want to leave but I can't rise from the chair. I'm tired, so tired. And the tears won't stop.

No, he says. Stay. I think you should stay.

He gets up and sticks the kettle on, makes coffee. He hands me a cup. I hold on tight with both hands and taste; no sugar.

He says, I'm going to take you up to see Maria Forbes. She's the student counsellor. You can't go home in that state. I can try to help, Lizzie, but Maria's better qualified and she can refer you to the medical centre. Maybe they'll give you something to calm you down. Drink your coffee and I'll give you a lift up there.

I say, I can't, Jim.

Yes, you can, he says. You must. I'll drive you there.

I say, No. I meant I can't drink this coffee.

Why not?

Because there's no sugar in it.

He smiles and hands me a bag of Tate and Lyle with a spoon stuck into it. I try to lift the spoon to my cup but I'm still shaking and granules cascade over his papers.

Here, he says, taking it from me. Let me help you.

We go downstairs and outside, past the curious stares of students lounging in the stairwells.

Where's he going with that woman? Did you see the state she was in? Maybe he fucked her and chucked her. It's always the quiet ones.

Nothing so glamorous, children. Lucky children: free to lounge and speculate on a Monday morning.

I can sense Jim's relief when he hands me over to Maria Forbes as if I was a lost child.

He says, Don't worry about your tutorial, Lizzie. I'll telephone you, and you can let me know if there's anything you need. I could always post articles to you.

Yes, I say. Thanks, Jim.

He says, Take care of yourself, Lizzie. Bye.

Maria ushers me into her room. I sit in one of the armchairs and pull the ashtray towards me. We sit in silence; me staring at a big box of tissues. I wonder how many of those she goes through in a week. Does she pick them up when she does her own shopping, put them on the list? Twenty boxes of man-size tissues. Would that be enough? And why 'man' size?

Maria sits opposite me. What does she expect me to say? I don't trust myself to speak.

I can't tell this nice lady with the tweed skirt and the wedding band how I really feel. I can't tell her about the terror. I am filled with terror. No, I wear it. It envelops me; stifling, suffocating. On the train, in the library, it drapes itself around my shoulders, and over my hair.

An inappropriate garment for the modern woman; belonging to an other age. The garb of the Victorian governess; the hysteric. I am cloaked in terror.

My demeanor betrays nothing, no emotion. I am unaffected. No anxiety, no panic. Panic leads to unseemly behaviour. I move smoothly through my days. I glide along in my protective clothing. Moving out, that time, past the authentic patrons of the Crennan Arms. Soundlessly, causing a minimum of inconvenience. Out into the air; composure and dress appropriate.

Here, I am afraid. I am afraid that they will see. Those brilliant minds. They feel my cloak brush against them. *What's wrong with Lizzie?* I don't want them to see.

The ones who have glimpsed my unstylish apparel sympathise.

How will you cope, Lizzie?

What has he done to you, Lizzie?

Christ, what a time for it to happen, Lizzie.

Defer, Lizzie. Defer.

No.

They push back the hood of my cloak. I feel foolish, exposed; a nun without her wimple.

I try the latest accessories: herbal teas, herbal tranquillisers, relaxation and meditation. They don't fit. Perhaps I should stick to outmoded fashions: sex, alcohol, and chemicals. The corsets that will hold it all in.

I can't be exposed. Exposed, affected, mad.

I say, Do you mind if I smoke?

No, go ahead.

She pushes the ashtray towards me. I wish that she would move those bloody tissues.

I wish that I could tell her. I want to say, You see, I can't use you. I can't use your big white tissues. Can't let go, you see. They need me. I can't cry. I can't scream. I didn't cry when she died. I won't cry now. I'm the mummy. I'm not unbalanced, unhinged. I never could be.

Is it cos I'm bad?

I want my mum and dad back.

She says, Lizzie, if you don't have the feelings, they will have you.

And at that I curl up in her big chair and howl big, broken-hearted howls; the way the weans used to. Wanting someone to hold me tight, wash my face, and tell me, There there, it will be all right.

But Maria only pushes the box of tissues closer, and waits for my outburst to end. Some mummy she is.

And then there's the telling.

Tell her about the crash, about my estranged husband and my poor, poor children. About my dear departed mother and my disapproving father. Now that the wall has crumbled, it all pours out.

I say, I could have been killed this morning. If the crash had been more serious, I could have died. And what would have happened to my children? Their father has no time for them; there is only me. I shouldn't be here, not now.

The tears flow on, pouring down my cheeks as I speak. She keeps up the supply of tissues, pressing soft white wads into my hands.

She says, I'll get my secretary to make us some tea. I'll be right back.

Her hand rests briefly on my hair as she passes. A gentle benediction. Thank you.

Alone again. How am I going to get out of here? How will I make the journey home?

She comes back, bringing a tray with cups and saucers, patterned with roses. Like the ones my mother had in her display cabinet. Never used, kept for best. Best never came, until her funeral.

Maria says, Lizzie, you have told me what has happened to you. What about your feelings? How do you feel?

Guilty. I feel guilty.

She says, What about sad, angry, upset, afraid?

I can't. How can I go on, if I have those feelings? I'll tell you what I feel. I feel lost. Up here, I was always Lizzie. And she was on top of everything. For three years she did it all; she coped with the travelling and the work and the family. And she looked good. And she was witty and smart, and one helluva woman. Now she's gone; I can't find her. And without Lizzie, I'm lost. I can't write essays, sit exams. Lizzie was supposed to do all of that. And my friends are Lizzie's friends. They don't know wee Mrs Burns from Saltcoats. And if they did they wouldn't like her. If I'm to go on I have to find Lizzie.

She says, But you are Lizzie. You are that strong, coping woman.

No. If I am Lizzie, then why can't I cope now?

She says, Because you are under immense pressure. Your husband has left you, you have three young children, and you are facing your final exams. Younger students without responsibilities crack under the pressure of exams, Lizzie. You have been expecting far too much from yourself.

Maria, my husband was absent most of the time anyway. I chose to come here, I made that decision. I should be the one who has to cope.

She says, Not alone. You need help. Do you have anyone to help you at home?

Yes, I say, I have a friend who helps me. And there's Lisa . . . my Lisa . . . oh I'm sorry.

I have become this pathetic, tear-sodden mass.

She says, Don't apologise. You need help, my dear. Will you let me help you?

I say, Maria, I'm lost, and I can't get home. How can I go back on the train? I'm so scared.

Don't worry, she says, someone at the medical centre will prescribe something to calm you down. What about your friends? Is there anyone who could go back with you today?

My friends. Would they understand? Lynne with her

paramours and her parrots. What would she think? And Tony? Take him back to my weans and my nice wee hoose? Oh aye, sure. Elaine. Elaine's the only one who would understand.

I say, Yes, Elaine Crossan. I think she'll be in the Social Sciences library, or in one of the coffee bars.

Maria says, Security should be able to locate her. I'll get Pat on to it. Now, let's get you along to the surgery. Just relax; I'll explain everything to them.

The doctor gives me some blue pills. Straight off, no prescription. I thought that someone would've had to go down to Boots in Byres Road. But no, I have them here in my hands. Foil strips with the days of the week written on the back, like contraceptives. No need for those now. I swallow Monday with another cup of Pat's tea. What will it do to me? Will it wipe away the memories, and all my knowledge with them?

To thee a woman's services are due. A fool usurps my body.

Or will I develop a passion for housewifery, spit and polish, vacuum and shine, become a Stepford Wife?

Impossible; I am no one's wife.

The guards have found Elaine. She is beside me, holding my hand saying, It's okay, it's okay, over and over.

My tears fall silently now, the harsh sobs have subsided.

I say, Will you go with me? Will you take me home, Elaine? Please.

Her arm encircles my shoulders.

Of course I will. And I'll stay and take care of the bairns. Don't worry, pal, we'll be fine, everything'll be fine.

She has taken to her bed, her big solitary bed.

I've lain here for ever. My solicitous friends bring me food and drink, and hushed words of comfort. The kids peep in occasionally. Bernie has told them that I have a virus; I need silence and rest. I have stopped crying, and thinking. The pills have done their job, but now I feel as if the top of my head is missing.

Elaine comes in, carrying cups of camomile tea for us both. She sits in the wicker chair by my bed.

How're you feeling?

Better, I think. But the pills make my head feel like cotton wool. I have to stop taking them; I'm going to need my head, all of it, if I'm going to sit my finals.

She looks at me, worried, then she nods.

Aye, she says, but you'll have to take it easy, pace yourself. And you'll need help. You can't do this on your own, Lizzie. I'll stay for another day or two, then I'll nip down as often as I can. And Bernie'll be here. We won't let you get into that state again. Okay?

Yes, I say, okay.

She says, I'm going out to the shops. Do you want anything?

No. But before you go, could you get my *Women Poets* for me?

She leaves me with plumped pillows and the heavy volume in my hands. Poetry in place of pills.

It was the pills that finally did for Adele and Sonia. Mummified with Valium, Librium and Mogadon; then Jumping Jack Flash on the Dexedrine; three weeks' house-work done in a morning.

What would you like to be when you grow up, Elisabeth?

I want to be just like you, Auntie. A sad, sodden divorcee, with my beauty and my hopes and my dreams all chemically erased.

And Sarah, Sky, whoever she was. I hardly bloody knew her but I know that she shouldn't have died. Did she swallow all the pastel-coloured calm drops from her pretty pillbox?

You're wonderful, Lizzie.

So were you, Sarah. So were you.

My mother's bedside table was littered with bottles of pills. Pills, and books of course, until she could no longer comprehend. And a photo of me in a cheap plastic frame. First communion. Little Elisabeth Mary, aged seven, gap-toothed smile and a squinty veil. Full of grace. My wedding photo never adorned her mantelpiece, but I could stick my graduation portrait on mine. Something to keep the weans away from the fire. Something to show that, unlike her, I had a life.

Close your eyes and think about nice things, baby.

No, Mum. I'm keeping my eyes wide open. I have to watch over my children, your grandchildren. And there are so many books I still have to read. I still haven't read Jim's dark lady, Djuna Barnes. I have to finish what you started, Helen. Love and literature. All I have. All that you left me. See, I'm opening the book, finding a poem:

'Instructions to the Double'.

What happened to my double? Last spotted striding through the station, groomed to perfection, shopping bags gripped in bejewelled fingers. I should have followed her. She wouldn't have been able to run away, not in those shoes. Where did she go?

Where are you, wee woman? I know you're out there, you, and millions like you. I'm not afraid of you now. In fact, you can do something for me. You can carry on. I have faith in you, I know that you can do it. You can gaze up into his eyes, and walk in high heels at the same time.

Yes. Keep it up, honey. You can do it all.

Shop till you drop. Replenish your supply of silky lingerie. Remain resolutely Rimmelled. Go on out there and strut your stuff. Do it for me. And I won't have to care.

I'll be too busy.

Here with the poets.

Taking the pain.

I wake up with the book lying open on the covers. No noise from downstairs. Where is everyone?

Bernie and my dad are in the kitchen. They both jump when I say, Where are the weans?

Bernie says, It's okay, Elaine's taken them to get a Chinky. You sit down. Tam, hand me a clean mug, will you.

My dad says, I didnie even know that you were ill. I phoned to see why you hadn't been down. I came up to see if I could help, but you've got your pals; you'll no need me.

I clutch the mug that Bernie hands me, warming through, before I reply.

Help, Dad? Well, that would be a first. All you've ever done is hinder me. Held me back, put me down, kept me in my place. You and Colin. But I have to study for my finals, you see. And no one is going to hold me back. You can help if you want. But one word of criticism, and you can follow the big man; you can fuck off.

He takes a step towards me, pain and shock clenched in his face.

Don't you dare talk to me like that. Your mother . . .

No. Not my mother. Me. This is not about her, and I am not her. The dressing gown's the only similarity. I won't lie down and die.

The tears again. Christ.

Bernie stands between us.

I won't let you upset her any more, Tam. She's had enough. She's right, you don't even know her. Take a look at that telephone pad out there. There are messages from all her friends, and her tutors. People that admire and respect, and care about her. And all she gets from her own father is abuse. Take a look at what you're doing, for Christ's sake.

The door opens, and David bounds in, swinging a carrier bag.

Yo, Mum. Hey, you two, Mum's up. Mum, we've been to the Chinky's, I mean the Chinese. We got loads and loads. Lemon chicken, and prawn crackers, and sweet and sour, and loads of rice. And Elaine got spring rolls, just for her, cos she's a veterinarian.

You mean vegetarian, son.

Sure, he says. I'll get the forks.

Lisa and Carrie cuddle up beside me.

Carrie says, Is your virus better now?

I say, Yes, hen. I think it's nearly better.

She says, Remember when you went to Auntie Bernie's party that time, and you were sick in the bathroom, and then you slid down the wall? You said you had a virus then. Was this a worse one?

Bernie winks at me. Yes, Carrie. I think this was definitely a worse one.

Elaine and the girls bring the food to the table. Lisa offers some to her grandpa. He looks over at me, expecting ... I don't know.

I say, You're welcome to stay and eat with us. But you'll have to take what's on offer; there's nothing else.

Taking the carton from Lisa's outstretched hands, he says, Thanks. I'll just have a wee drop. I've never had this stuff, but you don't know till you try, eh?

He turns to Elaine.

I'll gie you the money for all this, hen. Youse students canny afford it. I ken that.

ELEVEN

I am a student. I spend hours in my room, dissecting centuries of English literature. Coffee and sandwiches appear at my elbow, then my daughter tiptoes from the room, leaving me in peace. One day I will do the same for her. But these days are mine. Lizzie's.

I work, undisturbed, in the daytime. I cook the tea and make sure that someone else does the dishes, then I come back to my desk until one or other of them appears at the door.

Mum, there's a good programme on. Are you coming down to watch it?

And that's when I close the books, and go downstairs, because I know they still need me.

Last night I stopped in the hall, and read my telephone messages. One of them, in Lisa's careful handwriting, said,

Grandpa says he'll collect those two from school tomorrow, and take them to his house. I've to go straight there from school.We're having our tea there, and he'll bring us home at night.

My poor weans, he fries everything.

So, tonight I'm alone with Nora and Robin, in the wild worlds of *Nightwood*. I'm in the kitchen reheating leftover pasta when the phone rings. I consider leaving it unanswered, but it could be my dad. There could be something wrong.

I pick it up, and a terse voice says, Hello. What's happening?

Colin. He sees no need to identify himself. What other man would want to press my digits?

I say, Nothing's happening. Why?

Let me talk to the weans, he says.

You can't, they're down at my dad's.

What are they doing down there?

Having their tea. Spending time with their grandpa.

Oh, he says. So you don't even feed them these days.You just fob them off on to an auld man.

I will not do this. I replace the receiver. It rings again.

Fuck.

He says, Don't you dare hang up on me. Who the hell do you think you are?

Me? I'm aff ma heid, remember. I can be anybody I like. Queen Elizabeth, Eliza Doolittle, Betty Boop, Lizzie Borden. Aye, that's who I think I am, Lizzie Borden. You better watch, I might come after you with my axe.

You mental ...

This time I don't hang up. I gently place the receiver on the hall table. And I go into the living room and quietly close the door behind me, leaving him ranting into a cold, dark and lonely space.

Rave on, big man.

Saturday. Lisa's has been tidying up all morning. And when I ask her why she isn't out with her pals, she says she wants to stay in with me. Carrie disappears upstairs for a while, then shouts down, Mum, I've run a bath for you. I go up. She's even put bath oil in.

She says, I've laid out that nice cami top and knickers Auntie Bernie gave you at Christmas.

I say, But I'm only going to the shops. I don't think I need my nice underwear, Carrie.

She thinks for a minute.

No, she says. Lisa and me'll go to the shops for you. You stay in and have a rest. And put your nice underwear on, Mum. It'll cheer you up.

The wee soul. Have I been that much of a monster lately?

I've only been in the bathroom ten minutes, when she pounds on the door.

Mum, you'll have to hurry; I'm bursting for the toilet.

Downstairs, Lisa offers to blow dry my hair and paint my nails.

I say, But I'm not going anywhere. What are you two up to?

Nothing, she says. We just want you to have a nice day.

If it were my birthday I would suspect a surprise party or something, but that's not for weeks. If they've set me up with a blind date, I'll kill them.

The phone rings and Lisa sprints out to the hall. She comes back smiling.

It was a wrong number, she says. Why don't you put some make-up on, Mum? You look a bit pale.

The baker's van stops outside. The horn toots, summoning housewives out for Sunday breakfast tattie scones, and a nice cake for Saturday tea.

David looks up from the telly.

He says, Can I get sweeties from Mac's van?

And he runs to the window, anxious to get out before the queue forms.

Oh, Mum, he says, there's a big purple van out there. And it's got a big monkey wi knickers on. And my grandpa's getting out of it.

I say, David stop it. Sometimes your imagination is too much even for me.

There is, he says, jumping up and down. Look.

He's right. A purple Transit van, with a gorilla in pink lacy drawers painted on the side is parked at the gate. And my father has just got out of it. He's laughing and talking to someone. Christ, it's Tony. And there's Sean and Valerie, and Elaine, and a girl I don't know.

The wedding. I forgot about the wedding. Look at the state of them. Valerie's wearing a short shiny red dress, and her Docs. Her frock clashes with her magenta hair. And the other one. It must be her sister. She's all in black: dress, tights, and boots. And her hair, all piled up in black spikes. Elaine's wearing a granny's cross-over pinny, and a blue velvet cloche hat. The boys aren't too bad. Apart from the red ribbon in Sean's ponytail.

All the folk at the baker's van turn and stare. Mrs Niven from number sixteen is standing clutching a Mother's Pride, with her mouth hanging open.

My dad gives the letterbox a jaunty ra-ta-tat. I open the door and they all troop in.

My dad says, Bet ye wurnie expecting this. Heh heh. We're the talk o the toon the day, hen.

Sean grabs me.

Congratulate us, Lizzie. We did it. We're married.

I kiss them both.

Yes. Congratulations. But what the hell are you doing here?

Elaine says, Lisa phoned me. She said you were working too hard. So we've come to take you to the party. And now we're all here, we're not going back without you.

Now I understand what the bath and beauty treatments were all about. I look at Carrie and Lisa, they look delighted that their plan has worked.

I say, How did you manage to get David to keep his mouth shut?

Carrie says, We never told *him*. Do you think we're daft?

David sidles up. He gazes at Valerie and Tina, her sister.

He whispers, Are they real? Are they supposed to be in a pantomime?

Ignoring him, I say, But what about the kids? I can't leave them all night.

My Dad says, Aye ye can. Whit d'ye think Ah'm here fur? The wean phoned me, and we arranged fur the boys to pick me up.

It has escaped his notice that the van belongs to Tina, and that she was driving. I can't believe that he's agreed to all of this. He hasn't been this cheery since Saltcoats Vics won the Scottish Junior Cup.

I say, But I haven't got anything to wear.

That's easy, Elaine says. Here. We brought you a prezzie.

She hands me a star-scattered bag. Inside there's a dress. A beautiful pale-yellow dress.

Oh it's lovely. Thanks, Elaine.

I got it from that wee second-hand shop in the lane, she says.

Tony stops playing computer games with David.

Now that you're all out of excuses, will you go and get ready? The party can't start till we get there. Move yourself, Lizzie.

I go upstairs, hoping that David doesn't ask anyone what they're supposed to be. The dress fits perfectly. It's a nineteen thirties number. I look as if I'm going to a tea dance.

I come out of the bedroom and find Lisa waiting.

She says, You look lovely, Mum. Are you pleased? Are you pleased that I did it? I thought you might be mad at me.

I say, Oh no. I'm not mad at you, I'm very pleased, Lisa. Anyway, you're going to have to put up with your grandpa all night. God knows how he'll cope with David.

She says, I'll stay in. David behaves for me. And my grandpa's okay. He'll let us have our tea out of the chip shop. You better go down; they're all waiting for you.

I say, I really am pleased, Lisa. Thank you.

'S okay, she says. I like your pals. And that Tony's a bit of a hunk, isn't he?

Oh aye?

We fall about giggling at the top of the stairs.

Finally, we all troop out to the van. My dad hugs me on the doorstep.

Don't worry about the weans. We'll get wur tea oot the chip shop, and Lisa says she'll go fur a video. So that's yer pals? Ye didnae tell me wan o them's a Celtic supporter. Here. You'll need this fur fares the morra.

He slips a twenty into my hand.

Go and enjoy yersel. I jist want ye tae be happy, hen.

I know, Dad.

Well, he says, on ye go. Top o the pops. Hey, Tony, you make sure she has a guid time the night.

Will do, Tam, Tony says.

I climb in beside Tina. She drives off, tooting the horn. And I lean out and wave to my dad and the kids, still standing on the pavement. Just before we turn the corner out of sight, I wave one last wave to Mrs Niven.

The party is held in Valerie's parents' house, and it's like no wedding reception I've ever seen. For a start there's the guest list: girls in leggings and t-shirts, guys with beards and paint-spattered jeans. The bride's mother has cropped blonde hair, and four earrings in each ear, and her father looks like Richard Gere.

I stand in the kitchen with Lynne and Elaine. My living room would fit in here; the place is enormous. And God, the food: couscous, hummous, samosas, Cajun chicken, pates, salads, wild rice, wild mushrooms.

Elaine piles up another plateful and says, I'm really quite glad that Nick couldn't make it. There's a few total shags out there.

I say, I thought you were in love.

Lynne, predictably, bursts into a rendition of 'What's Love Got To Do With It?'.

Elaine says, So did I. But I think maybe I was just in lust. He bores me; all he talks about is bloody anthropology. If I do go to the States with him, he'll have me traipsing round fucking Navajo burial grounds.

Lynne says, Are you having second thoughts about the trip?

No, Elaine says. Oh no. With or without Nick, I'm definitely going.

She wipes away crumbs and drains her glass.

And right now, I'm going out there to dance, she says. C'mon, Lizzie. No more sitting in the kitchen at parties. You're going to have a good time.

Lynne says, That's right. Get out there and bag yourself a total shag.

I say, You're joking. I wouldn't know what to do with a total shag if I got one in a gift.

She says, That's an idea. If you don't click tonight, we'll get you one for a graduation present.

I haven't danced for ages, not properly. I bop about the living-room with the weans a lot, but that doesn't count. Here, I'm self-conscious, sneaking looks to see what everyone else is doing, until I forget myself and boogie on down like every other idiot in the place. I dance with Sean, and Richard Gere. His wife doesn't seem to mind; she's dancing hip-to-hip with Eddie, her body welded to his. Christ, he must think it's his birthday. I hope she appreciates honesty.

The music stops. Tony calls for order.

Thankfully, he says, I haven't had to do any of the usual best man things today. But I would like to propose a toast. Raise your glasses please, and drink to Sean and Valerie.

We chorus, Sean and Valerie.

Tony goes on, This is a great party, but there's just one thing missing: some traditional wedding music. This song is especially for Lizzie, the pretty woman in the yellow dress. Hey, Lizzie, you dancin?

He presses a button. And George Jones sings . . . 'Jambalaya'.

Tony puts his arm round my waist, and we sashay into a quick waltz, showing them how it's done, singing along with George.

The bride and groom twirl round beside us.

Valerie says, You having a good time, Lizzie?

Oh yes.

I can see Elaine, dancing with Sean's grandpa, struggling to keep his hands off her arse.

When the song ends we head for the drinks table.

Tony says, I've run out of fags. There's an all-night shop on Great Western Road. Fancy a walk?

I say, Yes. I could do with some fresh air.

It feels strange, being out at this time. The streets are still busy. People moving from pubs to clubs. Young couples entwined, taking the long way home. It must have rained earlier. I sidestep puddles in my strappy sandals; the only shoes that matched the dress.

I say, How come your girlfriend isn't at the wedding?

Tony says, What girlfriend?

I don't know. You've usually got one floating around somewhere.

No, he says, not for ages. I got really pissed off. You know, not one of them had a sense of humour.

I say, Meaning, they didn't find it funny when you fucked them and chucked them?

He says, Oh very clever, Lizzie. I've never done that. What I meant was . . . they seemed to think that being an intellectual and having a sense of humour are mutually exclusive. Everything's so fucking serious. At least with you and Elaine you can have a laugh.

Ah, but that's because we're over thirty. You will keep going for sweet young things, son.

He says, Lizzie, that's crap. Elaine looks about fourteen. And you would pass for early twenties any day. And you carry on like a pair of twelve-year-olds half the time. Why do you do that oh-I'm-positively-ancient stuff? Nobody gives a shit.

Jesus God Almighty. Another one. Another bloody man telling *me* who to be and what to do. I clench my fists, fighting the urge to draw my fingernails down his face, draw blood.

I say, Maybe for the same reason that you do that existentialist, tortured soul, working-class hero crap. Oh, go for your own bloody fags.

I turn and walk away. Stomping off, out all by myself in the dark.

Tony says, Lizzie, for Christ's sake, wait.

He touches my shoulders, turns me around.

I'm sorry, he says. I didn't mean to say it that way. What I meant was . . . I wanted to tell you that you're beautiful. You have to stop putting yourself down. You're terrific.

Still with his hands on my shoulders, he leans closer and kisses me. Suddenly I remember; remember how a kiss makes you clasp the nape of his neck, weave your fingers through his hair, move closer, feel the heat of his body warming yours. How just a kiss can leave you wet and warm and willing to melt.

What am I doing?

A wee bit of comfort, Lizzie.

Fuck the guy, no marry him, Lizzie.

He pulls me close, against straining black denim.

Oh.

His hands drop to my breasts, fingertips tracing circles through yellow crepe de chine. Car horns sound. Jostling groups of roaring boys lay claim to the streets.

Muscling in.

Get intae her, big man.

Fuck.

Are you pleased, Mum?

Are they real?

No.

I pull away but he grabs hold of my hands, holding tight. Ignore them, he says.

My knees are knocking, my stomach's churning, and if I

don't get a grip of myself I'll cry. I start gibbering like a budgie.

It's not just them, Tony. I'm sorry, but this isn't me . . . I can't do this . . . I just can't . . . I wanted . . . I thought . . .

Shh, Lizzie.

It's raining again, light spring drizzle smirring the lights along Kelvin Bridge. God. How did I get here? What the fuck have I done?

Tony says, No hassle, Lizzie. Tonight's your game, your rules. I'm not about to pressure you. I think you're beautiful. End of story.

Cupping my face in his hands, he looks into my eyes and says, Don't look like that. It's okay. C'mon, you're getting soaked.

He takes off his jacket, drapes it across my shoulders. I let him. We walk to the shop, and he buys cigarettes and a bottle of Jack Daniel's.

That lot'll have tanked all the booze by now.

I look at him, wet hair falling over his forehead, damp patches staining his shirt. Standing, smiling in the rain.

We'll get you one for a graduation present.

Anyway, he says, I could be doing with a stiff drink. How about you?

No, I don't think so. It goes straight to my head.

We arrive back just as Sean and Valerie are getting ready to leave. Everyone crowds out on to the pavement to wave them off. Elaine links her arm through mine, giggling and staggering down the steps.

I was about to call the cops, she says. You two were away ages. And don't tell me you just went for a wee midnight stroll in the pishin rain. Were you shaggin up a close?

Elaine! No, we were not. Shut up.

I look around. Tony's helping Sean load the suitcases into a taxi. I don't think he heard. She tries to hoist herself up on to the garden wall.

Aw, Lizzie, how no? Tony's fucking beautiful, an he's really intae you. He thinks— Whoops.

I haul her back before she lands arse for elbow in the rhododendrons.

I know what he thinks. Now get down from there, you'll break your bloody neck. Look, they're leaving.

We all gather round as Sean and Valerie climb into the cab.

Bye. Bye now. Have a lovely time. Good luck. Bye.

The driver toots his horn all the way round the crescent and out of sight. Elaine sits down in a puddle on the pavement.

Aw. Isn't it nice? It's just that nice. They're away to a hotel in the Highlands. And when they come back they'll live happily ever after. Sure they will, Lizzie?

Aye, hen. Maybe.

Exam time.

Like giving birth, bloody inevitable.

Bloody and inevitable.

If I register for the exams, there will be no going back. No hopping down from the delivery table. *Scuse me, could you hand me my knickers, please? I've decided not to bother.*

No pethedine, or gas and air. No tender young husband to hold my hand.

My other births were swift, and uncomplicated. But I was younger then. There are always risks with the older mother, when the mysteries of obstetrics and gynaecology run deeper.

Try to relax and get some sleep. I unclench my fists, but then find my hands pressed together, as in prayer.

Who would I pray to? Not God, the Big Man. I gave up on him when I sat in the back bedroom of my father's house, watching my beautiful young mother waste away. I didn't watch when they lifted her from the bed, and performed intimate nursing rituals. I made tea. It was all I could do. Not knowing that I would be lost without her, she had neglected to instruct me in the other womanly arts.

Why this? Why now? What I have never allowed myself to remember.

Ovarian cancer, almost impossible to detect. Until it became lethal. They opened her up, too late. She was sent home, all sewn up, neat and tidy. Sent home to become that howling, pleading creature, with only her pain to call her own.

When she died, her husband and her sisters went to Mass. But I, her only child, stayed away. I curled up in her chair and refused to move. And while they ritualised their pain with smells and bells, I anointed the pages of her books.

She had spent her housewifehood at the fireside; scorch marks patterned her legs while she read novel after novel. My father would complain that she had me as daft as herself. *It's no bloody healthy, Helen.* Then he would escape to the pub, leaving us in peace.

By the time I was ten, I had read everything in the junior section of the public library. They had to let me into the adult section, but the librarian censored my reading. *Forever Amber* was taken from me, put back on the shelf for years.

My mother showed me the only escape routes she knew. Books; words and imagination.

Close your eyes and think about nice things.

I prayed to her once. When David went missing I walked

the streets, intoning, *Mother, keep him safe. Mother, please watch over him*. I found him, standing transfixed by a tractor in the field. In the path of danger, but kept safe.

If I prayed to you now, Mother, would you hear? I thought that I could do this. But now I'm scared.

Close your eyes and think about nice things.

See yourself, a necklace of silver and jade replacing the choker of fear around your throat. A shawl of Spanish lace settling your hunched shoulders. Flowing silk smoothing over your stiffened body. Beautiful blossoms held in your unclenched fists.

Go to the sea. No, not the grey, rocky seaside.

In other places the sea is clear blue and calm. You have never travelled. But you will. You will go to the sea, and sit on the shore, and feel the sun on your face.

See yourself.

You will go to other seas, and other shores. You will live in other places, other rooms. On warm nights you will stretch out on a bed covered with fine linens, holding a warm, strong body in your arms, as words spoken in strange tongues drift up from the streets.

You will go on. You will keep going on.

See yourself.

You will go far.

When you're wired to the moon, Elisabeth, you can reach the stars.

The coffee bar is packed with ashen-faced wee souls, clutching last-minute study notes.

Up at the counter, Betty says, Coffee, hen? Yer wee pal's sitting up at the back, wi that big boy wi the ponytail.

I find Elaine, Sean and Valerie crushed in at a corner table. Sean is hunched over a *Collected Shakespeare*. His leg jerks under the table, spilling coffee, and Valerie jumps, mopping at her jeans.

Sean! Will you calm down?

Elaine moves along, leaving me a space at the edge of the seat.

Lizzie. Oh, you made it.

I say, What are you doing here? You said you didn't have a paper till Thursday.

I don't, she says. I'm here for you, pal. And I wanted to give you this. My mother sent it.

She hands me a tiny silver and blue medal. I turn it over in my hand, and gaze upon the face of the Blessed Virgin.

I say, I haven't seen one of these for years. It's a Miraculous Medal.

She says, I know. I should've asked her to send a box of them; we could all be doin wi a bloody miracle. Oh, and she says to tell you that she'll be saying five Hail Marys for you.

But I haven't been to Mass for years. Do you think that Mary'll listen?

She nods, smiling. Of course she will; she's not as narrow-minded as God.

Tony comes over. He crouches down beside us.

He says, I've forgotten who the fuck Coriolanus was.

I say, Mother: Volumnia; wife: Virgilia; otherwise: big tube.

Oh, thanks a lot, he says. That's a big help.

He leans closer.

I phoned your place this morning, but you'd already left.

Why did you phone me?

He says, Because part of me still thought that I'd be sitting there this morning looking at an empty chair where you should be.

He stands, puts his arm around my shoulders, and says, So, who are you going to be? The fainter, the hysteric, or the projectile vomiter?

All three. And I'll be sitting behind you.

Nutter, he says, grinning.

I look at my watch.

Oh Christ. It's time to go.

Sean jumps, spilling the remaining coffee.

Oh fuck. Oh fuck. Where are we going? I've forgotten. Where is it?

Tony says, The Great Hall. For Christ's sake, Valerie, get a hold of him, will you?

We walk towards the knots of shaking students gathered in front of the heavy oak doors. I see Rachel and Jim waving.

Rachel takes my hand.

She says, I knew you'd be here, Lizzie. Go for it. You deserve the Nobel Prize for fortitude, woman.

The security guard opens the doors.

Good morning, folks. Have your matriculation cards ready, please. Make your way up. Good luck.

Jim says, This is it, Lizzie Burns. Did you remember your axe?

I say, I remembered. You're a lovely man, Dr Brown. And he blushes. He actually blushes.

Elaine hugs me close.

Good luck. I'll be here when you come out.

We're moving. Sean walking backwards, his eyes fixed on Valerie's face. She raises both hands high in the air, fingers crossed.

Tony's beside me, his hand on my arm.

Lizzie. You know what?

What?

An orgasm would really lessen the tension.

The laughter rises, bubbling up into my chest. I keep it there, for later. We begin to climb. All those stairs.

Rubbing a little faith in miracles between my fingers.
Three
Four
Holy Mary
Breathing.
Ten.
Eleven.
Breathing.
Mother of God.
Nineteen.
Twenty.
Blessed art thou.
Breathing.
Breathing.
Among women.
Up there with the stars.
So high.
So high.